In a Small, Quiet Village
(Where Nothing Much Ever Happens)
The *Cities* & *Villages* Saga
Book I

IN A SMALL, QUIET VILLAGE (WHERE NOTHING MUCH EVER HAPPENS)

First edition. March 15, 2022.

Written by Ian Anthony Hollis.

Also by Ian Anthony Hollis

The Cities & Villages Saga
In a Small, Quiet Village (Where Nothing Much Ever
Happens)

Standalone
And so Began the War

Table of Contents

For Mum.

Written by
Ian A. Hollis

Cover Illustration & Design by
Meritxell Andreu
& Ferran Rodríguez

Prologue

A beautiful blue sky held white-and-grey clouds drifting high above the treetops, and a gentle breeze blew softly through the woodlands. A leaf carried by the breeze danced to the song of the wind calling through the trees, gently descending towards an unbeaten path.

Jacob was a brown-haired, hazel-eyed, energetic, and youthful ten- – almost eleven- – year-old with an energy one might describe as bright-eyed and bushy-tailed. He was out with his best friend, Sabrina, recently turned fourteen years old, whose eyes were like the colour of a cloudless sky, her flaxen-blonde hair like fields of wheat. Accompanying them was their mutual friend, Belle, the almost-nineteen-year-old town beauty, with hair like black silk that almost seemed to reflect a starry night sky, whose high cheekbones and deep-set chocolate-brown eyes somehow made her look mature for her age, and she had the height to go along with it

"Look!" cried out Jacob happily, pointing towards the falling leaf, a twinkle in his eye. "Another one. I can add this one to my pressed leaf collection too," he said as he held out his hand to catch the falling leaf. "Isn't nature wonderful?"

Belle smiled, holding her broad-brimmed hat to her head. "He sure is enthusiastic today."

Sabrina furrowed her brow and smiled. "He's enthusiastic every day, which you'd know if you came out with us more often."

Belle frowned a little and tilted her head as her eyes darted around and she pulled down the sides of her hat. "Uh, okay. Sorry about that."

"Why are you out here with us today anyway?"

"Actually, Angela asked me to come out and make sure neither one of you got up to any mischief."

"What? Then why come out here at all?" asked Sabrina.

Jacob spoke up. "Don't worry, it's just my mum being bothersome again. I know she does it because she cares, but sometimes I think she worries a little *too* much, you know?" Jacob pointed to himself and Sabrina. "We come out here and do this all the time, so I don't see why today would be any different."

"She told me not to tell you this," began Belle, "but she said she had an ominous feeling about today, although she couldn't really explain why."

As Jacob, Sabrina, and Belle ambled back to the village, the ground started rumbling. Jacob gasped, crouched down, and put his ear to the ground.

"The train!" he said, his eyes as wide as his smile.

"So what?" said Sabrina with a raised eyebrow and a smile. "The ground always rumbles when the train passes by."

"It's different this time. I can feel it."

Sabrina laughed. "What, you mean you have some sort of a premonition?"

"No, I can *literally* feel it through the vibrations in the ground. The train's stopping this time. Do you know what that means?"

Sabrina and Belle looked at each other plainly.

"Someone new's coming to the village!"

Jacob bolted back to the village in a tizzy of excitement, unintentionally kicking up a small whirlwind of dirt behind him, the girls having to cover their faces from the dust.

Adam's Arrival

Adam, a tall, well-built yet rugged young man, in perhaps his mid- to late twenties, with a scruffy head of hair and eyes that were neither a deep nor light shade of blue, stepped down from the steam train and took in the scenery of the exceptionally well-kept old wooden train station. He walked through the station, tipping his hat to the staff and other patrons as he continued onwards out of the station and onto the old dirt road. He headed off to his right to visit an old village he'd heard a lot about.

"Few people come back from that place, Adam," rang his grandfather's words in his ears. *"So, be prepared to settle down there if you ever plan to visit."*

The winding old road was considerably longer than Adam had prepared for, and on a hot summer's day like today, he was eternally thankful for the shade provided by the fully grown trees that lined both sides of the road. A white picket fence ran along the road to the left. Wiping his brow, he put down his duffel bag and sat by a tree, taking a swig of water from his flask. He leaned back against the tree, lowering his hat over his face, and closed his eyes.

An hour or so later, he woke up feeling remarkably well rested, adjusted his hat, picked up his belongings, and energetically continued on his way. The winding road rose and fell with the valleys and hills, the scenery barely changing from one stretch of road to the next.

This village I've heard so much about sure is a lot farther away from the train station than I'd expected, he thought as a train whistled far off in the distance.

"And when you've walked farther than you ever thought possible," rang more words in his ears, *"after you've emerged from the canopy of trees, look far into the distance, and there you'll see it. Like a beacon of hope. A light at the end of the tunnel. That small, quiet village where nothing much ever happens. Where you'll want for nothing, and ordinary people live ordinary lives. That place you're one day likely to call home. It's there, just atop a small hill at the bottom of a valley."*

As those words finished ringing in Adam's ears, he saw it. Just as his grandfather described. He smiled, walked onwards, a slight skip in his step and a song in his heart.

Children of all ages were having fun playing a variety of games in the streets. Games such as marbles, jacks, red light-green light, hopscotch, and so on, their parents watching them from the porches of their houses, making sure they were well behaved. One of the children looked up, noticing something off in the distance.

It was Jacob running back to the village as fast as legs could carry him.

"Mum, Mum!" he shouted again and again. "Grandpa. Grandma. Everyone! The train stopped. Someone new's coming to the village."

"My word," said Jacob's mother, Angela, in disbelief. "It's been such a long time since someone new came to the village," she added, just as her son had caught up to her. "Go and ask

Grandma to bake some cookies for whomever this new guest is going to be."

"When is Grandma *not* baking cookies?"

"Jacob. Go."

"Yes, Mum."

While the oldest couple in the village were only truly grandparents to a small handful of the children, they were affectionately known to everyone as Grandma and Grandpa, or sometimes Mr. and Mrs. G. They were both short and round, with grey heads of hair, and each had a rather jolly disposition. Their weatherboard house sat in not quite in the centre of the village and was painted bright red with white highlights.

"Oh, Jacob," said Grandma, taking her freshly baked cookies out of the oven. "Come in. You've arrived just in time. Adam'll be here any minute."

"How do you know his name?" asked Jacob, taking a plate from the kitchen cupboard to help Grandma put the cookies onto.

"When you've been alive as long as I have, Jacob, you become aware of so much more than what your five senses allow for."

"Okay," he replied, not really understanding what she meant.

Almost everyone had gathered at the edge of the village where Adam was approaching, the children happily musing amongst each other about what this newcomer was going to be like.

As Adam walked ever closer to the village, he couldn't help but smile, and seeing everyone gathered, he decided to give a big, slow wave of his arm.

"He waved," said many of the children excitedly, waving back, big smiles helplessly on their faces.

"Welcome to the village," said Angela, offering the plate of Grandma's cookies to Adam.

"Oh, thank you," said Adam as he took a cookie before taking a bite. "Wow, you're a great baker, ma'am."

"Oh, I wish I could take the credit," she said, a little embarrassed, "but these were actually baked by Grandma."

"Well, then my compliments to your mother."

"Oh, she's not my mother, but everyone here calls her Grandma."

"Oh, sorry."

"It's okay. Easy mistake to make. I suppose I should introduce you to everyone."

Jacob, being Angela's son, was introduced first. "This little dark-haired ten-year-old of mine is quite lively, very friendly, and easily gets lost in his own thoughts."

Next was Jacob's best friend, Sabrina. "These two have been best friends for as long as I can remember. Sabrina's family used to live in the next town over, but a few years ago, they moved here, and Jacob couldn't have been happier. And that flaxen-blonde hair of hers – I'm so jealous."

"*You're* jealous of *my* hair, Angela?" asked Sabrina, her eyes wide. "I would give *anything* to have naturally jet-black hair like yours."

"Maybe in the next life we can swap."

"Maybe."

"Anyway, those two girls over there eating lunch on the front steps of Grandma and Grandpa's house are Belle and Donna."

"The taller one's Belle," Sabrina pointed out. "And the shorter, rounder one is Donna. They're best friends too, just like me and Jacob." She called out to them to come over, but they didn't quite hear her, although they both waved, Donna far more enthusiastically than Belle.

"And these two here casually leaning up against the fence are brother and sister, Maxwell and Julie," continued Angela.

"Max, please," said Maxwell, coming over to Adam with an outstretched arm for a handshake.

"Hi, Max," said Adam, shaking Max's hand.

"Julius," called Julie, raising her hand. "You know, like Julius Caesar?"

"Got it."

"But Julie's fine too. You know, whatever."

"Okay, so it's ..." began Adam as he pointed to each person as he said their names "Julie, Max, Sabrina, Jacob, the two girls on the steps, and Belle and Diane."

"Donna," interrupted Jacob.

"Donna, right. And I don't believe you've given me your name, ma'am," he said as looked at Angela.

"Mum's name's Angela, but you haven't said your name either."

"Uh," Adam paused. "I haven't," he said, wide eyed. "The name's Adam. Nice to meet you all."

"Hi, Adam," said everyone.

"Of course," began Angela, "there are other people to meet in the village too, but for now, I think we should get you settled in. There's an empty old house at the back of the village by the road that goes down to the convenience store. We'll put you up there for as long as you like."

"You mean the *in*convenience store," interrupted Jacob.

"Jake. You know better than to interrupt."

"No, it's quite all right. The *in*convenience store, you say?" asked Adam, his head tilted slightly and an eyebrow raised.

"It's just so far away that it's really inconvenient to go there," said Jacob.

"Hence why we call it the *in*convenience store," added Sabrina.

"I see. You'll have to take me there one day."

"There'll be plenty of time for that later," said Angela, inserting herself back into the conversation. "Come on, Adam. Your new place is this way."

Angela, Jacob, and Sabrina all led Adam to his new abode, where he unpacked, felt unusually at home, and had one of the greatest night's sleeps he'd had in longer than he could remember.

Fearing the Journey

"Jacob, dear," Angela called out, "we're off to the city this morning to buy you some new clothes."

Jacob's face scrunched up as he threw the blankets off his face and rose out of bed. "Why can't we just get them from the inconvenience store?"

"They're out of stock for the time being, and they don't have a particularly big selection in the first place."

Jacob hated visiting the city. It was large, and it was loud, and it felt like there was always something happening, unlike in the village, which was small and quiet, where nothing *much* ever happened, and where he wanted for nothing. The only thing he wanted in the city was to get back to the village. Only the thought of being able to scoot around the department store on a trolley brought him any happiness whatsoever, much to his mother's dismay.

Trying to figure out a clever way of not having to go, Jacob asked if they could at least take the train.

"No, dear," his mother replied, "the train station's in the opposite direction from where we need to go, and I'm not entirely sure where the train goes, anyway ... nor where it comes from, for that matter," she said with a briefly raised eyebrow as she finished putting on her earrings.

Jacob sighed, got out of bed, changed out of his pyjamas into his weekend clothes, and joined his mother.

"All right, Jacob. Off we go," said Angela, as she ushered Jacob out the door and followed closely behind, shutting the door behind her, checking it was locked.

"I like this first part of the walk, Mum, but not so much the second," said Jacob, as they left the village and entered under the treetops towards the old train station.

"Try not to worry about it, Jacob. Nothing bad's ever happened to you on any of these walks, and I don't think it ever will."

After the old train station, but before the general store, Jacob and Angela took a left turn and walked deep into the woodlands, where the extraordinarily high trees and overgrowth cast such heavy shadows that it was a minute or two before people's eyes adjusted. With each step into and out of the broken light, Jacob could feel the cold touch of the branches' shadows clawing their way up his body as if they were hands grabbing at him, the soft whisper of the wind through the trees saying, *"Come hither, young Jacob. Leave your world behind you, and be one with the woodlands."* All of that, along with the road being remarkably and mysteriously well kept, always sent such a shiver both up and down Jacob's spine, such that he would always walk a step or two closer to his mother, holding her hand that much tighter during this part of the journey.

"Why are they asking me who I am? It's me, Jacob!" he yelled.

Angela giggled. "Jacob, that's just the sound owls make, like a cat says meow or a dog says woof."

"It just makes me feel spooked, like they have an ever-watchful eye over me or something, judging my every move."

Angela laughed. "It'll be all right, son. We'll be out of here soon enough. Look, we're almost at the end. You can see the light where we'll catch the ferry. You can even hear the splashing of the water."

"Oh," said Jacob, wide-eyed and anxious to be out of that part of the woodlands. "Can I go on ahead?"

Angela sighed with a smile. "All right, but you wait until I get there, okay? Not like last time. You had me worried out of my mind last time."

"Okay, Mum. I'll wait, I promise. Okay?"

"Okay. Go," she said, ushering him off.

Jacob ran towards the light as fast as he could, making extra sure to wait for Angela when he got there.

Reading a Book

Belle was lying on her bed, face up, reading her book of short stories while Donna, who'd decided to come visit for a few hours, was puttering around Belle's bedroom doing this and that and looking at what sorts of things Belle had purchased since last she was there.

"Sit still already, Donna. All of your puttering around is so distracting. Just sit still somewhere."

Donna plonked herself down on the bed, right beside Belle, making the mattress bounce, which annoyed Belle just a little. "What book are you reading?"

"It's just a book of loosely connected short stories."

"Yeah, but what's it called?" interrupted Donna before Belle had finished speaking. "Like, what's the title?"

Still holding the book above her head, Belle closed the book, placing a finger between the pages so as not to lose her place.

"*In a Large, Loud City (Where Something Almost Always Happens)*," she read aloud.

"So, kind of the opposite of this place, then?"

"Yeah, I guess, but ..."

"But what?"

"There's just this one thing I don't understand."

"Tell Donna your problem! Donna will *save the day*," she said, punching the air emphatically.

"Well ... I get that these characters are all in the same city, and some characters even appear again in different stories, which is nice, but ..."

"But what?"

"I don't know if all the stories will come together in the end, unifying everything that's happened, or if they will stay forever separated as individual stories. I think it'd be really nice if they all came together. Heart-warming, almost."

"Have you checked the contents page?"

"The contents page?" retorted Belle. "That'll just tell me what page each chapter is on. For example," Belle flicked through the pages to find each chapter and page number, "chapter one, page twelve; chapter two, page thirty-five; chapter three ..."

Donna again abruptly interrupted Belle before she could finish. "Aren't you even paying attention?"

"What do you mean?"

"Look here at each chapter," Donna pointed out as she flipped the pages back to the beginning of each chapter. "Each chapter has a subheading. For example, chapter three is called 'Woody and Wesley—Finally Found,' which means the contents page will probably list the chapter's subheading and give you a clue to what's going to happen, so if you look at the title of, say, the last three chapters, that should give a clue as to whether or not all of your beloved characters will finally meet. What, are you expecting there to be a wedding or something?" asked Donna as she snatched the book from Belle's hands, flipping through the pages to see if she could figure out who she thought Belle suspected was going to get married.

"Hey, give it back." Belle struggled with Donna to get the book back, which Donna found quite humorous. "You can borrow it when I've finished!"

"Okay, fine," said Donna, loosening her grip on the book.

Belle and Donna were now lying face down, the book open on the pillows in front of them. Donna pointed out that what she'd suspected about the contents page was quite true. "See? It's here."

"Oh, I see," said Belle while closely looking over the page. "And the final chapter is called?"

They turned the page and noted that the final chapter was called "All Together Altogether."

"Yep," began Donna, still holding the book, "I guess that means they all end up meeting in the end, huh?"

"Yeah, I guess."

They looked at each other, paused, and then laughed.

Donna stayed on Belle's bed, closed her eyes, and became lost in her thoughts while Belle kept reading the book.

Meeting Amanda

Adam woke up the morning after he arrived, feeling as refreshed and rested as could be. While he was in his kitchen preparing his oatmeal for breakfast, he heard someone puttering around outside in his backyard.

"Hello?" he called out as walked out his back door and saw a woman, presumably around his own age, tending to the garden.

"Oh, hello," replied the young woman, as she stood up, turned towards Adam, and smiled. "I'm Amanda. I'd heard someone new had come to the village. I didn't think I'd be meeting you so soon. I didn't wake you, did I?"

She had long, straight, black hair; porcelain-white skin; large brown eyes; and a million-dollar smile.

"No, actually, not at all. I'm an early riser," said Adam, trying to simultaneously sound impressive and casual in the same breath. "What are you doing here?" he asked as he attempted to contort his face into what may have been the world's most awkward smolder.

"Oh, sorry," she said as she stood up and brushed herself off and turned towards Adam. "I can leave. Um, is your face okay?"

Adam realized how ridiculous his clearly failed attempt at a smolder must look. "It's fine, actually," he began, as his face returned to normal. "I'm just wondering what you're doing.

This place is far more your village than it is mine. I only arrived here yesterday afternoon."

Amanda explained to Adam that each of the villagers took turns tending to this particular house's gardens, as it didn't previously have a tenant in it, and today was her turn. "Honestly, I love nothing more than tending to these flowers, and no one minds that I do it more than I'm supposed to."

"So, because this house was empty previously," began Adam as he sat down on the steps, "everyone just takes care of it together?"

"Oh, very much so. I think Jacob and Sabrina and few others will be along in a few days to paint it," she said as she gestured towards the chipped-off paint.

"Wow. I love that this place has such a strong sense of community."

"It's been that way for as long as I can remember."

"So, you've lived here your whole life?"

"Yeah. I was born and raised here. I honestly haven't seen much more of the world than what this place has to offer, but I love it here so much, why would I ever want to leave? Why would anyone?"

"It's certainly an exceptional little part of the world you've got yourself here," said Adam, looking around at the trees that covered the road towards the old train station, also commenting on how thick the bushland is.

"Yeah. There's a small river back there somewhere that for some reason you can hear more clearly at night."

"Everything's quieter at night, I guess," mused Adam.

"Oh, and I love no nights more than I love a night lit by a full moon. In summer especially, we villagers are often up much later under the light of a full moon than on other nights."

"Hey, would you mind showing me around? I only met a few people yesterday and don't really know which houses belong to which people."

"Actually, Mrs. M, Sabrina's mum, is planning a lamb roast dinner the evening after the house is painted, and everyone's invited. You and I can go together if you'd like, and you'll have a chance to meet the main characters then."

"The main characters?" asked Adam with a contorted smile.

"Well, yeah. I kind of think of this place like a book. Everyone's their own main character in their own stories, and supporting cast in everyone else's stories."

"And what does that make me?"

"I guess that makes you ... a special guest."

"Right. And how long until I'm supporting cast?"

"I guess we'll find out at the dinner I just invited you to."

"Okay, then. I'd like that," said Adam, finishing his oatmeal before heading back inside. "Just let me put this in the sink, and I'll be right back out."

"I'll be right here. Oh, and don't tell anyone else about the book thing. It's kind of a *me* thing."

"A *you* thing," said Adam from the kitchen window.

"Yeah," she replied, fidgeting with her hands and looking every which way but at Adam.

Adam was now having real difficulty controlling his laughter. "A *you* thing that you've never told anyone, ever, until now, for some reason?"

"That's pretty much it, so," she said as she pressed her upward-pointed right index finger against her lips.

"Right," said Adam with strong affirmation. "So, mum's the word."

Amanda nodded.

"You're secret's safe with me. I'm actually gonna go unpack just a little more."

"Sure. I'll see you around."

"Great, see ya."

Adam closed the kitchen window and went about his business.

Cowering Before Giants

The intolerable din of the city streets always had Jacob on edge. His face scrunched up and his shoulders tensed as various and unfamiliar things made a wide variety of various and unfamiliar noises, people of all shapes and sizes rushing past him.

"Jacob," said Angela, "I know the city's not your favourite place, but it can be just as good as the village if you're willing to open your eyes to it. Look over there for example." She pointed to some boys running along the street, playing with sticks and hoops. As Angela noticed them bump into and push each other over quite intentionally she told Jacob, "Well. Maybe that style of play's not for you. Come now, Jacob. The department store's just up ahead."

"I wish Sabrina was here."

"Sabrina has sports today with Kevin, not to mention some extra tuition this afternoon to help her with her academic pursuits."

Angela realised how on edge Jacob seemed, and she tried to comfort him with a reminder of tomorrow's activities painting the side of the old house which Adam had moved into. "And Sabrina will be there also, painting right along with you."

Much to Angela's relief, this seemed to relieve Jacob's tension. His eyes lit up, and a gentle smile crossed his face.

"May I go play in the toy section?"

Angela paused, a blank expression on her face as she quickly glanced about the store. "All right," she said with a relieved although subtly tense sigh. "I'll meet you at the entrance in around ... fifteen minutes?"

"All right then. Thanks, Mum," he said before scampering off to play in the toy section of the department store.

Throughout the toy section lay large displays of various toys, and Jacob had seen a hobbyhorse. His eyes widened slightly.

"Excuse me, sir, may I ride on that hobbyhorse?" asked Jacob of one of the nearby shop assistants.

"Go ahead, lad. That's what it's there for."

"Thank you, sir."

After only a few moments of Jacob having been on the hobbyhorse, some slightly older but much larger boys came along. The largest in particular of them forcefully stopped the hobbyhorse and asked Jacob what he was doing.

"I'm just riding the horse. The man said I could."

"What man?" asked the boy, stepping uncomfortably close to Jacob.

"Uh," said Jacob has he looked around. "He's not here anymore."

"Well, maybe you should get of it, then?" said the boy. "Ain't you too old for this sort of stuff, anyway?"

"Or maybe," started up one of the other boys, "he should stay on it, if you know what I mean."

"Yeah, maybe he should stay on it."

The boys started pushing the horse back and forth, holding Jacob in place.

"Whoa! Now hold on, boys, doesn't you think we's bein' a bit rough?" said the oldest boy as he noticed the hobbyhorse starting to crack.

"*We's* bein' too rough?"

"Well, maybe it's not us at all," said one of the other boys. "Maybe it's this wee lad here."

"Yeah, maybe it is," said the oldest as they all snickered. "Go on then, off with you."

Jacob climbed off the horse. "But I was just –"

"You was just *what* then, mate?" said the oldest boy, punching his fist into his other open palm. Jacob gasped, turned around and, shaking, hurriedly walked to entrance, where his mother was hopefully waiting for him.

At the entrance of the store, Jacob met up with his mother. "Jacob, where have you been? I've been worried sick about you!"

"I was just playing in the toy section," replied Jacob, visibly upset.

Angela scoffed and told Jacob not to get upset just because she was cross with him for being late.

"Come on, Jacob, we're leaving," she said as she grabbed his hand and hurriedly walked off. Jacob didn't care that she was cross with him; he was just relieved to be going home.

Painting a Wall

The following day, not long after breakfast, the sun was peeking just above the treetops, with a light mist in the air. Sabrina and Jacob were getting ready to paint one of the outside walls of the old house in which Adam was currently staying. Jacob told Sabrina of yesterday's woes. "Gee, you sure don't have much luck when you go into the city, do you?"

"I *hate* it over there. I like it here where it's quiet."

"I like that about the village too. Maybe just forget about that, and let's get on with painting this wall."

"Right!" said Jacob as he and Sabrina picked up the various tools for the job. Now armed with paint cans, rollers, and a paint tray, they were ready for anything.

"How do we get up to paint the bits we can't reach?" asked Jacob, pointing towards the roof.

"With a ladder, dummy," Sabrina nicely replied.

"Oh, yeah."

Sabrina and Jacob looked at each other, rollers in the air, trying not to laugh, and said in unison, as they always did before starting a project together, "Right. Let's *do* this!"

Sabrina enthusiastically started painting, covering as much of the wall with as little of the paint as possible, while Jacob hesitated.

"Wait a minute."

27

"What's wrong, Jake?" she said, still enthusiastically painting the wall, doing an unexpectedly good job.

"What if the wall doesn't want to be painted?"

Sabrina stopped dead in her tracks, took a deep breath, and huffed just a little. "What do you *mean*, 'What if the wall doesn't want to be painted?' It's a *wall*."

"Well, we can't know whether or not it wants to be painted. I mean, yes, it clearly *needs* to be painted, but what if it doesn't *want* to be painted? We can't know its feelings."

"It's a *wall*, Jacob. It doesn't *have* feelings."

"Don't say that, Sabrina, you'll hurt it's, um, feelings," he said awkwardly.

"Okay, Jacob, look – if it *was* capable of processing thoughts and feelings, it'd be feeling and thinking one thing and one thing alone, okay?"

"And that would be?" said Jacob with a raised eyebrow.

"Yes, Jacob," continued Sabrina harshly, "it would be thinking and feeling." She paused, arranging her body like a wall. She squatted slightly, faced Jacob squarely, and partly stretched her arms out by her side, bent at the elbows so her hands were pointing downwards.

"Wall," she said, "and that is *all* it would ever think *or* feel *forever*. It's a *wall*."

Jacob stared blankly at Sabrina for a moment or two before suddenly bursting out laughing at just how silly he realised he was being. "I guess that is kind of stupid, isn't it?"

"Yeah, now can we just get back to painting? I'd like it done before lunchtime."

"Um, yeah."

Jacob started doing his fair share of the painting and asked Sabrina if she knew whether Kevin would be joining them later.

"Nope. Kevin's going over to Belle's place this afternoon. I think they're meeting at Grandma's place."

They painted and painted and painted. Eventually, after all that painting, they needed a ladder.

Sabrina asked Jacob if he thought Julie and Max still had that sturdy, old ladder in their shed.

"You mean the one we used to pretend was a pirate ship?"

"Yeah, that's the one."

"I'll go find out."

"No need to, kids." Max's voice came from around the corner as he and Julie appeared, each holding a ladder.

"Grandpa'll be here in just a minute with his long, sturdy plank of wood," said Julie.

"What for?" asked Sabrina.

"That's easy," remarked Max happily. "We'll set up these ladders a good distance apart, then, instead of each one of you having to lean over to paint the wall from your individual ladders, we'll put the plank between the ladders, so you'll have a shared platform. It'll be less awkward that way. Just be careful to not accidentally kick over the paint."

After the two ladders and plank had been set up, Sabrina and Jacob climbed up to where they needed to be and got back to work painting the wall, with Sabrina painting much more enthusiastically than Jacob, although Jacob certainly wasn't complaining.

A few hours later, the wall was finally finished, shining a bright white, reflecting the late-morning sun.

"Whew. We're done," said Jacob before he climbed down the ladder.

"Sure are."

Sabrina climbed down, put the lids back on the paint cans, and they washed off their brushes and hands under the faucet at the back of the old house.

"Now we just have to pack everything up, clean ourselves off, go home, change into clean clothes, and we can get on with our day."

"What about the two ladders and this plank of wood, though?"

"Ah, don't worry about these. Max said he and Julie would come by either later this afternoon or probably tomorrow morning to fix it all up."

Sabrina noted that the paint wasn't all used, so she put the lid back on, pressing it all over the rim to make sure it was on nice and tight. "It might come in handy for something later."

"Mine's empty. I'll just throw it out." He did so in a trash bin at the corner of the building.

"Okay."

Sabrina and Jacob looked around, making sure they were as packed up as they could be.

"Looks like everything's fine," said Jacob.

"Sure does. I hate the smell of fresh paint, though," said Sabrina, her face scrunched up.

"I don't like it either. Hey, do you wanna come over for dinner later?"

"Oh. Nah, that's okay, Mum's cooking my favourite tonight. Roast lamb!"

"Roast lamb? Can I come over to *your* place for dinner tonight?" Jacob's face lit up.

Sabrina giggled and agreed that it should be okay. "So long as your parents are okay with it."

Jacob's mother came by, appearing from the back of the old house. "Oh, here you are. I thought you might have been around the other side of the house, but Max and Julie sent me around here. How are you both?"

"We're good, thanks, Mrs. H. How are you?" replied Sabrina.

"I'm fine, thank you. Jake, your father wanted me to tell you that we're going over to Sabrina's family's house tonight for some roast lamb. Is that okay with you?"

"Hell yes!" he said, quickly covering his mouth in shock, realising he wasn't supposed to swear.

"Jackie, no swearing now, okay?" his mother said emphatically. "Anyway, we'll be heading over at around seven, so Dad wants you home by five, okay?"

"Okay, Mum. See you at five."

Jacob's mum headed off.

"*Yes!*" said Jacob excitedly, turning to Sabrina and giving her a high-five with both hands at the same time. "Looks like I'm coming over anyway! I'm gonna go home and get ready *now.*"

Before Jacob almost ran off in an excited rush, Sabrina said to him, "But what are you going to do in the meantime? Dinner's *hours* from now."

Jacob paused. "Oh, hey yeah. Well," he began, his arms outstretched, his hands upturned, his facial expression contorted. "Then ... now what?"

"Well ... we should both go back home and get changed out of these dirty, paint-covered clothes and into something clean. I'll meet you in front of the Town Dinner Hall afterwards, and we'll go for a wander down to the Inconvenience Store and get something to eat."

Jacob and Sabrina both headed off to their respective homes, cleaned themselves up, changed into clean clothes, and re-met in front of the Town Dinner Hall before heading off to the local inconvenience store.

Having Lunch

Belle puttered around the kitchen as she looked in the cupboards and the fridge, wondering what to eat for lunch on the steps of Grandma's house when her mother, Sandra, suggested that she just have some of last night's spaghetti Bolognese leftovers.

"Oh, thanks, Sandy. That's a great idea."

Sandra folded her arms and looked at her daughter. "Are you calling your mother by her first name again, Belle?"

Belle smiled, trying not to laugh, and responded with, "Well, it's not exactly like you call me 'daughter', is it?"

"Get out of here," replied Sandra, as she whipped Belle's backside with a tea towel before she left the kitchen to go elsewhere in the house.

"Hey, I can't leave before my lunch is heated up," said Belle right before the timer went off.

"*Now* you can leave," her mother called out from the living room where she was dusting.

"When I've put it in the container and got myself a fork I can," she said, as she did those very things. "Okay, Mum, I'm off now. See you later."

"Goodbye, *Daughter*," said Sandra to try to annoy Belle, but to no avail as Belle just left the house laughing.

Darting around the kitchen, Donna picked up one fruit after another to place on the island bench to start cutting up for her fruit salad.

"What are you doing, dear?" asked her mother.

"Preparing a fruit salad for lunch with Belle."

"Oh, you and that Belle girl do get along ever so well."

"Of course, Mum, she's my best friend. Now where's the knife?"

"It's in the top drawer like always, dear."

"Of course." She smiled as she opened the drawer, picked up the knife, and diced the fruit.

"Oh, honey, you're not going to put yogurt on that again, are you? You remember what happened last time."

Donna laughed and thought that yogurt sounded like a great idea, getting some out of the refrigerator as soon as she heard her mother say it, and laughing as she remembered the mess she made previously.

"It's fine, Mum, don't worry about it," she said before readying herself to head out the door.

"Do you have something to eat it with, dear?"

"Oh!" Donna went back into the kitchen and grabbed a spoon and a fork before again returning to the door. "Got it. It won't be like last time," she said, laughing again at the memory of what happened last time and the mess that it caused.

"All right then, dear. You say hi to Belle for me now, okay?"

"Got it, Mum. Say hi to Belle for you. See you!"

"See you."

Donna shut the door behind her and went off to meet Belle.

Belle and Donna often sat on the front steps of Grandma and Grandpa's house to eat their lunch.

Belle always sat on the porch with her feet sharing the middle step with Donna, whose feet were flat on the ground.

Belle was eating the leftover spaghetti Bolognese from her lunch container, and Donna was eating the fruit salad she'd prepared earlier.

Snapping open the lid of the small, rectangular container, the aroma of the previous night's reheated spaghetti gently drifted upwards towards Belle's face, and as she took a deep breath in, she delighted at how good it truly smelled. Neither too raw nor overcooked. Her mouth watered with how scrumptious it would undoubtedly taste, its texture in her mouth neither too meaty nor too saucy, the spaghetti neither too stringy nor too chewy, with the perfect amount of cheese added on top.

"Mm ... my cooking is *so* good," said Belle.

Donna laughed a little and replied, "Don't flatter yourself, honey. But yeah, it smells fantastic. I admit you're a really good cook. But for me right now, there's nothing more delicious than this," she said as she pointed at her lunch.

Donna had brought her fruit salad in a small, round tub, which contained chunks of watermelon, apple, orange, grape, pawpaw, cantaloupe, and honey melon, every last one of them sweet and moist, dripping with the freshness of the morning dew. "And it's made all that much better by the soft, milky texture given to it by this yogurt I've put on top of it too. It's *so* good."

"Is the fruit from your father's orchard?"

"You mean the couple of trees and vines in the backyard he likes to *call* his orchard."

"Won't he get mad that you used them before he had a chance to make his famous cordial? I love that stuff."

"Nah, he won't get too mad. A little annoyed maybe, but not mad. And why *wouldn't* you love his cordial? It's famous for a reason," she said sternly.

"Mm," agreed Belle.

The cordial made by Donna's dad was famous because of his uncanny ability to mix the perfect blend of syrup and water, never too weak or too strong, but always exactly the perfect mix of both. Always extremely refreshing for everyone who ever tried it, regardless of who they were or where they were from.

Donna continued, "Other than the cordial, he also makes jams and sauces, and all sorts of different things, even soda."

"Soda? How?"

"He just goes and buys some carbonated water from the store. It's the only bit he doesn't do from scratch, and then he squeezes some juice into it and sweetens it with sugar. In fact, when I was younger, he used to tell me that he'd stick his bum in a bathtub full of cold water and fart in it, and that's how all the bubbles got in there. He told me that's how all sodas were made. It completely put me off soda until I read an article in the paper explaining how it was actually made. I was quite angry after that, having believed my father's lies."

"And how do you feel about soda now?"

"Ah, I don't mind it every once in a while. In fact, all this talk about it has kind of made me feel like some," she said, standing up. "Would you like one as well?"

"Lemon flavour, please," replied Belle, nodding, still enjoying her spaghetti Bolognese, savouring every delicious bite.

Donna walked into the front hall of Grandma's house, where the entrance to the right led to the kitchen and the one to the left led to the living room, where Grandma always sat in her favourite dark-green velvet-covered recliner, knitting furiously away.

"Grandma," Donna called out, "may I take a soda?" She powered straight towards the fridge.

"Yes, that's fine, dear. Make sure to take one for your friend as well, dear, okay?"

"Thanks. I'll take a creaming soda for myself, and Belle said she'd like lemon."

"Oh, don't take the lemon one, sweetie. Grandpa's saving that for after work, and there's not many of them left."

"Excuse me, Grandma, but it looks like Grandpa's made a new batch. There's like, twelve of them in here."

"Oh. Well, if that's the case, feel free to take what you need. Are they warm or cold?"

Donna reached into the fridge and grasped a few of the bottles to make sure, and it seemed that the few she checked were all cold. "They're all quite cold, Grandma."

"Even the ones at the back?"

Donna rolled her eyes at the pointless questioning and without checking answered, "Yes, Grandma, even the ones at the back. In fact, *especially* the ones at the back."

"Ah, that's good to hear. All right then, dearie, carry on."

Donna took the two drinks and went back outside.

"Here you go," said Donna, handing the lemon soda to Belle before sitting back down on the middle step.

"Oh, thank you."

"You're welcome. Oh yeah, I meant to mention something just before we got side-tracked onto soda."

"Side-tracked?" Belle whispered to herself.

"Dad's strawberry-muffin pancakes are to die for. He makes them for breakfast sometimes and serves them with cream."

"They sound nice."

"They are. If you're not doing anything, you should come over and try them sometime."

"Okay. I'm usually up quite early, exercising with Kevin, so I can come over tomorrow morning after that, I guess. Is around eight okay?"

"Perfect."

Some clouds lazily passed high above the village as a gentle breeze passed by, softening the intensity of the midday sun. Donna noticed clouds looming ominously on the horizon and asked Belle if she thought it would rain later. Looking off toward the horizon, Belle simply answered, "Yeah," accompanied by the distant sound of rolling thunder.

Belle ate. Donna drank. The conversation stopped, and together they enjoyed what remained of the midday sun.

Finding a New Pair of Shoes and Walking to the Inconvenience Store

Sabrina hurried home, excited that Jacob would not only be coming over to dinner that evening, but also going to the store with her a little later.

"Mum, I'm back!" she called out. "Where are my shoes? Jacob and I are going to the Inconvenience Store this afternoon."

"Oh, honey, get washed up before going out, okay?"

"Yeah, I was gonna go have a shower, but can you please find my shoes so they're ready when I get out? Thanks."

Mrs. M, with a smug smile on her face, looked in her shopping bag on the kitchen table and thought, *Won't she be surprised to see these?*

She got a shoebox out of the bag.

"Huh?" she thought aloud, lifting the box "This seems unusually light." Looking in the box, she felt like her blood froze. "Where are the shoes?"

"Harry!" she called out to her husband, whose name was actually Sam. "Have you seen those new shoes I bought for Sabrina?"

"Ha-ha-ha. Why am I only Harry when you want something?" He smiled, puffing on his pipe.

"Oh, be quiet, Sam. Have you seen Sabrina's new shoes or not?"

"Hm," he said, taking his pipe out of his mouth, pausing for a moment's thought. "Pink and matte silver, as I recall. White shoelaces."

"Yes," replied Mrs. M, perking up, "those are the ones."

"Hm ... let me think."

"Oh, Sam, you and your bloody thinking. I'll find 'em quicker if I look for them myself."

"Oi, oi, oi," said Sam calmly, waving his hand in front of him. "There's no need for that. I think I put them out the back. I'll go look for them."

"I'm done with the shower," called Sabrina, as she came barreling down the stairs. "Have you got my shoes, Mum?"

"Ah, one moment, dear. Your father's gone out the back looking for them now."

"But I wanted you to have them ready *now*," complained Sabrina. "Like, so I could just put them on and head out the door. I'll just wear my old sandals."

"Oh, heavens no, dear."

"Why not?"

"Well truth be told dear, I—"

"Found them," Sam called out from the back.

Mrs. M breathed a sigh of relief, knowing she wouldn't have to spoil her daughter's surprise by outright telling her what she'd bought.

"Sabrina, I hope you don't mind," began Mrs. M, as Sam brought forth the shoes he'd found, "but I've gone to the liberty of buying you a new pair of shoes."

"Um, thanks but ... those are my old shoes."

Mrs. M turned to look at the shoes and scolded Sam for getting the wrong pair of shoes after he'd claimed he already knew what the new ones looked like.

"Mum, it's fine, it doesn't matter. I'll just wear—wait a minute."

Sabrina gasped in excitement. "You mean the new shoes from—"

"Yes, those are the ones."

"Oh," Sabrina added sheepishly. "Ah ... the pink-and-white ones?" she asked, even more sheepish still.

"Sabrina. Have you got something to tell me?"

"They're in my closet," she answered, shying away from eye contact.

Mrs. M breathed a sigh of relief, before becoming slightly fretful. "Oh, thank God. I thought I'd left them on the boat or the tram or the bus or the train or the taxi or something. All right then, dear, go and put them on and go and have fun with your friend."

"The ... boat?"

"Huh? Oh, sorry. You know I say all sorts of weird things when I'm in a fret."

"Yeah, okay. Anyway, I'm off," she finished, before heading upstairs to put on her new shoes.

"Don't forget the shopping list on your way out, sweetie. It's pinned on the corkboard by the door."

"Okay."

Jacob sat on the front steps of the Town Dinner Hall, waiting for Sabrina to show up, knowing she wouldn't be too far off. He sat there in his dark-blue shorts, his white T-shirt, and his new light-brown shoes that were slightly too big for his feet. His mind wandered from one subject to another, such as to how he could improve his grades at school, what would happen in the next action-packed issue of his favourite Saturday morning comic strip, what exactly Kevin would be doing with Belle this afternoon, and would Donna be with them as well? His mind slowly drifted back into reality as he heard someone running towards him who sounded slightly out of breath. He knew all too well that it was Sabrina, but for some reason, her running sounded a little different than usual.

"Do you like my new shoes?" she said, showing off her new baby-pink-and-white sneakers.

"Those are *girls'* shoes!"

"I *am* a girl."

"Oh, yeah. Right. I suppose you want me to tell you how nice I think they are, but really, they're just shoes." He shrugged.

"I thought you'd be a *little* bit more enthusiastic about them."

"Why would *I* be enthusiastic about *your* new shoes? They're *your* new shoes, not mine."

"Oh. I guess you've got a point. Well, I'm gonna be as enthusiastic about them as I like."

"Yeah, go right ahead," said Jacob as he laughed lightly.

"Shall we go?" they said in unison.

After they were just out of the village on the old country road towards the Inconvenience Store, Jacob asked, "So pink's the colour of the day, huh?"

Her shorts and the writing on the back of her white hoodie were also pink.

"Oh, you noticed?" she said happily. "Yeah, I just did some quick exercise before I came so I'd be nice and energetic for the walk, hence why I was a little late. Sorry about that."

"No, that's okay. I was off in all kinds of a daydream when you came running up."

"I just did some exercises I remembered Kevin showing me. I wonder if Adam's any good at things like that."

Jacob shrugged. "You'd have to ask him."

"Oh, hey, do you mind if we stop in at the old train station and get a drink?"

"It's fine by me."

The old train station, which had stood there abandoned for many a year, was about a third of the way between the village and the Inconvenience Store, closer to the village. It was an old, dilapidated wooden building that used to be an off-white cream colour, but it was hard to tell from how badly weather torn the building had become over the years. These days it was basically nothing more than broken windows, cobwebs, old bird nests, and overgrowth. And yet, what was basically a tin-roof shed still stood, and inexplicably contained a perfectly working vending machine. No one knew who put it there, who refilled it, or who maintained it, and yet there it stood in all its glory. A perfectly working vending machine.

"So, let's see here," said Sabrina as she eyed off the different options. "Do you want something?"

"No thanks."

"I think I'll get an apple juice," she said, inserting her coins and pressing the according buttons.

Jacob and Sabrina continued down the road, both starting to be a little more cautious when the road entered into bushland and was covered by trees that had not been tended to for all too long of a time, if they'd ever been tended to at all.

"I don't like this part of the walk," said Jacob. "I prefer it when I can see the sun and the sky."

"I dunno. I kind of like it, hearing all of the different bird calls and all."

"Well, I'll still be happier once we're out of it and on the other side, closer to the store."

"Scaredy cat," she said plainly.

There followed a time of silence, not because Jacob had felt awkward after being called a scaredy cat, but because Jacob and Sabrina had a secure enough friendship to know that not every second of space needed to be filled with words.

After a while Jacob made an inquiry about the train station.

"I don't actually know anything about it," replied Sabrina. "Although I seem to recall being there once when I was very young and seeing a train. It was a cream-coloured train with a horizontal blue stripe all the way along it, as I remember. It was old and clunky. But they tell me it hasn't operated for more than fifteen years, and I'm not even that old, so I don't know why I remember it the way I do."

"Memories are funny like that."

"Yeah. Ah! The convenience store. It's in sight."

"You mean the *In*convenience Store."

"Oh, yeah. That too. I'll race you."

"Can we wait till we get a little closer first? I don't really feel like running down a slope then up one. This is such a hilly walk."

"All right, we'll go from that telegraph pole over there."

The second they approached the telegraph pole, Jacob bolted off towards the store, leaving Sabrina with a face full of dust.

"Hey!" she shouted, running after him. "You didn't wait for me to say, 'Ready, set, go' yet."

"How am I supposed to beat you if I don't give myself a head start?" he yelled back.

They ran and ran and ran, and surely enough, Sabrina started catching up to Jacob all too quickly.

"Your shoelaces!" she called out, noticing that they were starting to loosen. "They're coming undone."

"So?"

"If you're not careful," she added, now almost by his side, "you'll trip and fall."

"Not me!" His two last fateful words before his shoelaces tripped him up and he fell over, slamming his knee into the front stairs of the store. "*Mother of ten gods!*" he screamed, tears streaming uncontrollably down his face.

"Are you okay?" asked Sabrina, crouching down beside him, making sure he wasn't too badly hurt.

"*I hit a fricking nerve.*"

"Hey, what's all this ruckus going on out here?" asked Mister Jones, the kindly old store owner, as he came out to investigate the noise. "Ah, it's you two kids from the village. Sabrina and Jacob, if I'm not mistaken."

"Hi, Mister Jones. We were having a race, and Jacob's shoelaces came undone, and he tripped and fell and banged his knee."

"Yes, I heard. I felt the whole shop shake. Come inside, and we'll get you cleaned up."

"Here's my mum's shopping list," said Sabrina, reaching into her pocket and handing it to Mr. Jones.

He smiled. "Ah, thank you, Sabrina, but I think you're old enough now that you can find all of those items by yourself."

He handed the shopping list back to Sabrina and took Jacob behind the counter, where there was a sink and a first-aid kit to tend to Jacob's knee.

"Done," said Sabrina, placing all of the items on the counter.

"Okay then," said Mr. Jones, ringing up all the items on his rather old-fashioned till. "That all comes to a grand total of sixteen ninety-five."

Sabrina gave Mr. Jones the exact change and Mr. Jones said, "Somehow I don't think this is all for your mother."

"Ah, no. I feel bad about what happened to Jacob, so I got some extra stuff."

"Oh, that's not necessary," said Jacob.

"No, it's fine. We'll go sit around the side of the building in the sun where we normally sit to go and eat it. It'll mean there'll be less to carry home that way."

"Okay then." Mr. Jones smiled. "You kids go off and enjoy yourselves. I'll be right in here if you need anything. And you be careful about that knee, Jacob."

"Yes, sir."

Jacob and Sabrina went around the side of the building, sat down in their usual spot, and started digging into the chips, drinks, and ice creams that Sabrina had bought, talking about anything and everything, including quite a lot of nothing. Sabrina ate. Jacob drank. The conversation stopped, and together they enjoyed the mid-afternoon sun.

"We should head home soon if we wanna be back in time for Mum's lamb roast dinner."

"Yeah. Not to mention before it starts raining," added Jacob, as he noticed the accumulating clouds high above the trees becoming progressively darker.

Sabrina also looked up. "Good point."

Waiting for the Storms

Amanda was standing on her front porch, her hand wrapped around the back of her head to control her hair from being blown around too much by the gentle breeze. Adam had his arms folded in front of him for the same reason, but for his clothes, not his hair.

"I hope those kids are back by this afternoon," said Amanda, looking out at the horizon.

"Oh? Why's that?" asked Adam.

"The storms are coming."

"Oh, I don't believe I've met the Storms yet."

Amanda giggled slightly, realising the mistake Adam had made.

"Did I say something?"

"No, it's just that I mean actual storms," she said, pointing towards the distant horizon where the clouds were a threating grey and the whoosh of the winds through the trees could be heard, along with the sound of rolling thunder in the far, far distance.

"Oh," said Adam in a moment's realisation "The *storms* are coming. Got it. Sorry, it's just that I've been introduced to so many people since I've been here, I just assumed–"

"Yeah, I know," replied Amanda with a smile. "But to tell you the truth, they do have names."

"Okay," said Adam, not sure how to respond.

"No, I'm serious." Her smile dropped and the mildly playful tone in her voice was no more. "They're brother and sister. Johnathan and Summer."

"Oh, you're serious."

"Yes."

"And *Summer* Storms? Really?" he said, clearly questioning the obvious play on words. "Who's their cousin? April Showers?"

Amanda forced a smile at Adam's jest and went on to describe that Summer is the smaller of the two who lightly dances through streets, bringing with her gentle, short-lived showers. But Johnathon was a force to be reckoned with. Strong, heavy, stubborn and relentless.

"If you ever see Johnathan Storms," she said, "get inside, close the doors, shut the windows and pray to God that everyone else is also safe in their houses."

"That bad, huh?"

"Yep."

"And what do you mean if I see him? How can you tell which is which?"

"Occasionally," began Amanda, "usually around this time of year, someone will see a young woman wearing a pink dress adorned with a floral pattern and a broad-brimmed straw hat, dancing through the streets. But no one ever gets *quite* a good enough look at her to know what she *really* looks like. She comes in through one of the entrances to the village and dances on through the streets and then makes her way out of town, never to be seen nor heard from again until the following year. Usually within the next few days is when the storms begin."

"You mean I might *actually* see someone?"

"Sort of, but not quite."

"It doesn't sound too bad, to be honest. Now tell me about her brother, John."

"Johnathan!" she snapped, explaining that calling him anything other than Johnathan is bad luck, and she didn't want to mention him any further, as legend has it that describing him will summon him.

"Right, so if I see a lady dancing through the streets, but don't *quite* see her, everything should be fine, but if I see, I guess from what you've told me, some big burly bloke, I should be worried, right?"

Amanda nodded. "They could come together, one by one, or even weeks apart, but usually it's just one or the other."

"Got it."

"Just remember that if you ever see Johnathon Storms that the closest house is the safest house to be in."

"Again, got it. So, fingers crossed for seeing Summer this year."

"Here's hoping."

"Anyway, I'd best get going. Grandma and Grandpa invited me over for tea later."

"Oh, it'll be a treat. Save some of Grandma's cookies for me."

"Will do. See you later."

"See you."

Carting Back to the Village

Jacob and Sabrina hadn't walked far when Jacob's knee started playing up because he'd banged it earlier. "I really don't think I can make it all the way back to the village, Sab. I hit my knee *really* hard. Like, you have no *idea* how hard."

"Well, I guess it did shake and reverberate through the wooden structure of the store quite strongly when you banged it. I did wonder if you'd be okay to walk back again."

"Oi!" called Mr. Jones. "You kids, come over here. I've got something for you."

Jacob and Sabrina looked at each other and made their way back to the store, wondering what it was that Mr. Jones had in store for them.

"I couldn't help but notice your limp as you wandered off, so I thought you could do well with this."

Mr. Jones took them to the shed around the back of the store where he presented them with an unpainted but well-made billycart from his childhood that was in almost-perfect condition.

"But Mr. Jones," began Sabrina, "this is one of your most prized possessions. We couldn't take this from you."

Mr. Jones offered a kindly smile and a gentle laugh and told Jacob and Sabrina that his reaction wasn't much different when he was first offered the billycart by his best friend's grandfather when he was just a young lad. "My friend at the time had an injury and was suffering badly from the flu. I was his choice for driver if he wasn't able to make the race, which, because of his condition, he wasn't. So it was me who ended up entering—and winning—the race for him. Sadly, he died from health complications around a week later, and his grandfather entrusted me with this very billycart."

Taking in the story Mr. Jones had just told, Jacob ran his hands over the billycart, appreciating not only the fine craftsmanship that had been put into the cart but also its history.

"Mr. Jones, you're so kind," said Sabrina, appreciating his sacrifice.

"No, it's okay, really. In fact, this one's been specially modified to help carry groceries too. I used it quite a lot for that, back when I was younger. So, Sabrina, given that Jacob has a bad knee, you should be the one that stands at the back."

"You mean I get to steer?" said Jacob excitedly.

"When you get to an uphill incline, the cart will slow down, so it's up to the person at the back to jump off and push as much as possible, and I don't think you'd be able to do that with your bad knee, Jacob."

"I'd make a better pusher than Jacob anyway, Mr. Jones."

"I agree," began Jacob. "You're *way* pushier than I am."

"Hey!"

"All right, all right, you two. Please take your positions. Wait. Let's make this official," said Mr. Jones as be pulled out a checkered flag on a stick as if from nowhere.

Sabrina blurted, "Hey, how did—"

"On your marks ..."

Hearing the seriousness in Mr. Jones's voice, Jacob and Sabrina scrambled into the positions on the billycart.

"Get set ... *Go!*" called Mr. Jones, dropping the flag. Sabrina immediately began pushing the cart as fast as she possibly could.

Jacob, as it turned out, was quite competent at steering the billycart, no doubt from all of those hours 'practicing' with shopping trolleys in supermarkets when he accompanied his mum into the city. And Sabrina was a more-than-competent cart pusher. However, the billycart hadn't been used in so long that all the pressure and force being exerted on it by these two lively young children was beginning to take its toll on this old, no longer frequently used billycart.

"It feels like it's starting to fall apart," Sabrina called out.

"Yeah, I know, I can feel it starting to buckle."

"The train station's not that far ahead. Do you think we should stop when we get there?"

"Keep going. I'm pretty sure we can make it."

The billycart thundered and rumbled along the road back to the village at an increasing pace. The road from the train station onwards was a very slight downward incline, and the cart was already going at quite an impressive pace, only picking up more and more speed as it rumbled onwards.

Both Sabrina and Jacob cried out in fear as they began approaching the village at all too incredible of a speed, both a little worried that they might have a head-on collision with something, or worse, *someone*.

Jacob decided to aim the failing cart for the road in front of the Town Dinner Hall, as that was the widest in the whole village, and by the time the cart had come to a complete stop, little more than a long, wide plank of wood remained, on which Jacob and Sabrina had basically just surfed into town. They'd managed to stop exactly in front of the Town Dinner Hall's front steps, and when they looked up, they saw Grandma standing there.

They weren't sure if she looked shocked or angry, and then she finally just burst out laughing. "You two are always having so much fun together."

Preparing for Dinner

"Gee, that lamb roast sure does smell good," said Julie as she and Max casually wandered in through the open front door to Mrs. M's house.

"Oh, Julie and Max," said Mrs. M as she stuck her head out the kitchen door into the living room to see who was there. "Please, come in and help me here in the kitchen if you wouldn't mind."

"Yeah, no worries, Mrs. M," said Julie happily as she and Max wandered into the kitchen.

"Julie, if you wouldn't mind cutting up what's left of those vegetables," said Mrs. M, pointing to a specific, prearranged pile of vegetables, many of which had been sliced already. "And Max, if you wouldn't mind dicing *those* vegetables," she continued, pointing to a different pile of vegetables.

Julie and Max happily lent a helping hand each, knowing that Mrs. M, especially when it came to cooking for large crowds, wasn't known for her organisational skills in the kitchen.

"So, how've you been, Mrs. M?" asked Max.

"Oh, heavens, Max, I've been running around like a chicken with its head cut off. All this preparing for tonight's meal, making sure I've got enough stuff and all the right ingredients, darting back and forth to the store and so on. Just this afternoon, I had to ask Sabrina to get something from the store for me, but she was going with Jacob anyway, so it was a trip not wasted."

Someone else shouted from the front door.

"Hello?" It was Benji, the tallest girl in the village. "I've just come back from sports practice. Is it okay if I use your shower? It's closer than my place, and I've got all my stuff with me."

This time it was Julie who stuck her head out the kitchen door, smiling and waving at Benji as Benji smiled and waved back.

"Tell her it's fine, Julie."

"Yeah, it's okay. Mrs. M says it's fine."

"Thank you!" Benji called out, rushing up the stairs to have a shower. "Is anyone else here yet?" she yelled from upstairs.

"No, honey," answered Mrs. M.

"You're actually kind of early!" shouted Julie. "But they'll all probably be here by the time you've come down from the shower."

"Okay, thank you. See you in about forty minutes or so."

"Forty minutes?" asked Max. "Surely, it shouldn't take more than ten?"

"We girls are different to you boys. We need extra time," said Julie.

"For what?"

"We're just more thorough. You boys get in, get wet, get out, dry off, and get dressed."

"Yeah. That's all you need to do."

"Yeah, but us girls actually care about how we look and feel. Sometimes I think you boys only shower because society expects it of you."

Max thought about that last statement for a while before answering. "True. I shouldn't have to shower if I don't want to."

Adam knocked on the open door with Amanda in tow and knocked again before shouting out a hello to see if anyone was home.

"Oh, Adam and Amanda," said Sabrina's mum, rushing around the kitchen trying to get far too much done in far too little time. "Please come in and set the table if you wouldn't mind. Max and Julie are here helping me in the kitchen already."

"No worries at all, Mrs. M."

"Please, call me Angelina."

"The same as Jacob's mother?" inquired Adam.

"No, Jacob's mum's Angela, I'm Angelina."

"Oh. My mistake. Sorry."

"No worries. It happens."

Over the past few hours, Adam and Amanda had become well acquainted, and deep down they shared a mutual respect. They had different pasts, different life experiences, and didn't quite see eye to eye with one another but always tried to appreciate and understand each other's differences. One way that they didn't see eye to eye was in the setting of a table. Amanda had little experience setting tables outside of the village, save for the occasional big trip to the city to see distant relatives, whereas Adam had experienced many different varieties of setting tables and various formalities from one family home to the next. Setting this table was going to be an impossible mission with both Adam and Amanda competing to set the table the way they each saw fit. It was a mad rush to see who could prepare the most places at the table as neatly and quickly as possible before either one of them had a chance to get more places done than the other.

Once they'd finished, they told Sam, Sabrina's father, who, upon looking at the table said, "Where on Earth did you guys learn to set a table? Not a single one of those is correct."

Adam and Amanda felt like they'd been deflated like old balloons.

"Never mind about this," said Sam. "I'll fix it. You two go and round up the kids. Dinner's almost ready, anyway."

The kitchen was hot from the oven, which brought an unwelcome heat on this midsummer's evening. Outside, however, was a considerably more pleasant temperature, the sun starting to hide behind the tall trees, which cast a cooling shadow over much of the village.

Belle and Donna, along with Sabrina and Jacob, waited outside so as not to overcrowd the living room or the kitchen, for Julie and Max were helping Sabrina's mum prepare dinner, while Adam and Amanda were preparing the dinner table. Benji was in the shower, and Kevin hadn't arrived yet.

Belle was wearing little more than some flip-flops, denim short-shorts, and a bright-pink bikini top under a white singlet. The heat of the day, coupled with the hard work she'd been doing with Kevin just before showing up to Sabrina's house, had made her quite sweaty, causing her singlet to stick to her body.

"Jacob, what's wrong?" asked Sabrina as Jacob was unusually silent with his back turned. He was pretending to admire the flowers in Sabrina's front yard, but he never admired flowers.

"Uh ... nothing," he said, as he turned his head towards Sabrina, but just didn't quite make eye contact with her, then turned away again.

"Seriously, Jacob, what's the matter?" she asked again as she went around to face him. He was fidgeting with his pants in an unusual way. "Oh ... um ..."

"I don't know why, but my pants start to get uncomfortable when I'm around Belle these days," he said, fidgeting more with his pants, in an attempt to make them more comfortable.

"Oh," she said in realisation. "Just Belle, though, or some other girls too?"

"Uh ... Belle and Donna," he whispered, "and sometimes Benji."

"Okay. Just relax, okay?"

"Yeah, but, it's awkward and uncomfortable."

"You know what? I've got a pair of old boys' pants that I used to wear that I think would fit you. They should be a little looser fitting than those pants."

Sabrina took Jacob up to her room, ruffled through her clothes looking for the pants she mentioned, threw them over to Jacob, and said that she'd wait for him downstairs while he changed.

Sabrina, who emerged from the front door onto the porch, talked to Belle, who was sitting on the front steps eating a lemon flavoured ice-lolly, and told her that her parents would probably expect her to dress a little more formally than what she was wearing.

"Oh, really? They've never had a problem with it before."

"Ah, it's the new guy."

"Adam. I was there when he showed up."

"Yeah, Adam. My parents are just hoping that everyone will be dressed respectfully for his sake. You know, more covered up?"

"More covered up? Ah, I wish other girls weren't always so jealous of my natural beauty."

"It's not that." Sabrina sat down on the cement step next to Belle and whispered in her ear, "I think Jacob has a crush on you."

Belle opened her eyes and looked at Sabrina. "Really?" she said, smiling. "That's cute."

"It's just that he's just at that age where ..." began Sabrina, struggling with how to explain it, before just saying "His pants get uncomfortable when he's around you."

"So, he should get new pants," replied Belle, as cold and as sour as her ice-lolly.

"Yeah, he's up in my room right now putting on some of my old pants."

"Great, so what's the problem?"

"Because he's at that age where his pants will almost always get uncomfortable around you, if you know what I mean."

Belle thought it over for a moment. "Oh!" she said, in a sudden moment's realisation. "Okay, I'll go put on something more conservative."

Belle got up from the step and asked Donna if she was going to come along too. Donna, who was wearing a bandanna, a bikini top, a slightly oversized heavy white shirt with silver studs for buttons and two chest pockets, some denim board shorts, white socks, and sneakers, wasn't much more conservatively dressed than Belle.

"It's okay, I'll just wait here. Jacob's pants get uncomfortable around you, not me. I'll just do my buttons up before I go in."

Belle glared at Donna with the intensity of a bolt of lightning.

Donna, with an eyebrow raised, looked back at Belle. "What?"

Belle stormed off, and Sabrina sat down next to Donna, who asked Sabrina about the afternoon's wall-painting activities.

"Ah, it was okay, I guess," she said, before telling Donna that she also had to put up with Jacob's strange philosophy of the wall not wanting to be painted.

"He's funny like that, isn't he?"

"Yeah, he is. He seems to think all inanimate objects have a state of being other than what they really are."

"Yeah, I know. But I guess that's just his way."

"Yeah."

"Hey, where is Jacob, anyhow?"

"Um," she said, looking around. "I dunno, I'll go check."

A little while later, Sabrina realized that Jacob was taking an unusually long time for just changing a pair of pants and decided to go up to her room and check on him.

"Hello?" she said, knocking on her door. "Are you decent?"

"Come in," said Jacob.

"What in the world are you doing?"

Jacob turned around, holding a black shoe in one hand and a shoe-polishing brush in the other. "Polishing this old pair of shoes. They looked like they were feeling sad and lonely for the little attention they'd obviously been getting. And plus, I thought doing something else would take my mind off Belle, so I started polishing these shoes."

"Oh, I thought ..."

"Thought what?" replied Jacob, puzzled.

"Nothing. Um, just wanted to tell you that dinner will be ready soon. We should go downstairs."

"Okay," said Jacob happily before he put down the shoes and brush. "Let's go."

Over dinner Adam got to know the villagers, parents and children alike, and started to feel more and more like this was the sort of place where he could definitely settle down for a long time.

"Oh, Adam," said Mrs. M, "will you be participating in the autumn festivities in a few weeks?"

"Uh, I don't know," replied Adam, awkwardly looking around at people. "Will I?"

"Of course, you will," answered Grandpa. "There's no reason not to be."

"Benji here arranges the whole thing herself," continued Mrs. M, "and everyone pitches in as best we all know how. It happens over at the Town Dinner Hall."

"The Town Dinner Hall?" asked Adam curiously.

"Well, it doubles as the town hall and is also where we have dinner as a large community when absolutely everyone comes to eat. It's fantastic."

"Sounds like fun. I'll do anything I can to help."

"I just hope we don't have any trouble with bad weather," said Grandpa, an almost-blank stare on his face.

"Oh, you mean Johnathan and Summer Storms?" asked Adam.

"So, Amanda told you about them, huh?"

"She sure did. Just earlier today, actually."

Joshua, Jacob, and Sabrina

F ar from the village, a rooster crowed at the crack of dawn, announcing the newly risen sun. A new dawn, a new day. And once again it was as ordinary of a day as the village had ever experienced.

Joshua was a tall young man in his early twenties with a curly mess of short, rusty, red hair; fair skin; and a light spray of freckles across his face. Behind his mysterious yet soulful green eyes and friendly smile stood a sense of warm-hearted mischief. He stood at the front of his porch, with a far-off look in his eyes, hands in his pockets, and fidgeted with whatever was in his pockets and stared off towards the exit of the village that led towards the Inconvenience Store.

"Hi, Josh," came a voice from off in the distance. It was Jacob with Sabrina, walking back to the village, each eating an ice cream.

"Oh." Joshua skipped down the stairs, smiled, waved, and walked over to meet them. "You two sure are up early."

Jacob smiled, laughed lightly, and looked at Sabrina.

"We stayed the night at Kevin's place," said Sabrina.

"Yep. And Mister Jones lets us help stock the shelves in the morning if we're early enough."

"He *lets* you?" asked Joshua.

"Yeah," said Jacob happily.

"Well," said Sabrina, "he pays us in food, as you can see," she finished, gesturing towards the ice creams.

"He said he writes it off as a, what did he call it? A five-finger discount."

Joshua laughed heartily "A five-finger discount? He said that?"

"He sure did," smiled Jacob.

"Jacob," began Sabrina, "it means —"

"It means," interrupted Joshua, "that after you two have put in a little bit of hard work for Mister Jones, he pays you with free food, and that's basically all there is too it."

"Speaking of food," began Jacob, "we didn't see you at Adam's welcome banquet last night."

Joshua momentarily dipped upwards on his toes before falling to his heels, put his hands in his back pockets, and stretched his back, chest, and arms. "I was up all night studying, I'm afraid."

"Studying? But you're a grown-up. I thought grown-ups had jobs."

Joshua laughed. "That's certainly what they want you to think."

"Who's *they*?"

"Um ... er ..." Joshua looked around and folded his arms, uncertain of how to answer.

"So, what are you studying, anyway?" asked Sabrina.

"Oh. Theology and spirituality."

"What's theology?" asked Jacob.

"It's just another word for religion."

Jacob turned his head, squinted, and leaned away ever so slightly. "I sometimes think you grown-ups are up to something. What are you *really* studying?"

Jacob, with a far-off look in his eyes once again, set his gaze beyond the exit of the village that led towards the Inconvenience Store far from the old train station.

Sabrina turned around briefly, also looking towards the exit. "What are you looking at?" she asked before turning back around.

"To answer Jacob's question, I'm studying religion to see if I can decipher if there really is more to this world than what we can perceive with our five senses."

"Do you think there is?" asked Jacob.

"I hope so, Jacob. I hope so."

"Well, it'd be a boring old world if there wasn't."

Both Sabrina and Joshua laughed.

"You mean something like life after death, right?" asked Sabrina.

"Yes, but not just that. Not just life after death, but life beyond life. That which lies beyond the here and now."

"So, the 'there and then,' then?" said Jacob with a smirk.

Joshua laughed. "I like your way of thinking."

"You keep looking off towards the bushland with a certain look in your eye. Will you be leaving soon?" asked Sabrina, her lips ever so slightly aquiver, water faintly welling in her eyes.

Joshua's face became expressionless, and he gave the slightest of nods. "We'll see."

"Well, let us know before you go, okay, and we'll arrange a big send-off like we always do when someone leaves the village."

"You know what? This is all getting a bit much. How about a game of cricket?"

"Can it wait till just after lunchtime? Mum'll get mad if I don't return when she expects me to."

"Not a problem. Let's play at the old playground behind Grandpa's place."

"Deal. See you then. Bye Josh, bye Sabrina."

The three of them each went to their respective homes and bade the time until lunch.

Dining with Mr. and Mrs. G.

A few days after the dinner gathering at Sabrina's parents' house, Adam decided to visit Grandma and Grandpa.

"Knock, knock," said Adam as he knocked on the wall beside the wide-open door, as there wasn't really anywhere else to knock.

"Oh, Adam!" said Grandma, placing a tray of freshly baked cookies on the table. "Just in time. Please come in."

"Come in, old man, come in. Good to see you again!" called Grandpa with a smile on his face, placing down the newspaper that he'd been reading.

"Ah, hi again," said Adam as he entered through the front door and into the kitchen. He looked around, unsure of where to sit.

"Oh, just sit anywhere," said Grandpa. "That chair's closest to you, so why not sit there?"

"Will do," said Adam, taking a seat at the table. "Well, those cookies sure do smell good."

"Oh, and I'll bet they taste every bit as good as they smell, if not better. Help yourself."

"I think I'll wait until they've cooled down a bit first."

"Suit yourself. Sorry I wasn't here last time. I was out getting some firewood for the old fireplace," said Grandpa as he pointed out the fireplace. "So, you're new in town, huh? Tell us a little bit about yourself."

Adam told Grandpa of his life as a wanderer, moving from one town to another, never quite finding the right place to settle down, always eventually moving on from one place to the next. "The time always comes, you know? No matter what, one way or another, the time to move on always comes eventually. For better or for worse."

"Huh. So, you're a well-travelled man. I used to do quite a bit of travelling myself when I was younger."

"Oh," interrupted Grandma, "and what travelling have you ever done since you got here?"

"Well, you're the reason I stopped travelling and settled down here. I travelled aplenty before you and I met."

"Oh, go on then, tell your stories."

Grandpa spoke of his youth and how he and his friends would travel together from one place to the next, some eventually going their own way, not to be seen again, and some settling down. "And then eventually, there was just me, wandering from place to place until I came here, met this woman, and decided to stay. I just *knew*, you know?"

"I know," replied Adam. "But somehow doubt always seems to find me."

"I understand. Just give it time, wait it out, and see what happens."

The shutters on the windows suddenly started flapping lightly in the breeze, and everyone turned their attention to it.

"Oh, that's never a good sign," said Grandpa. "Looks like it's probably gonna be Johnathon this year."

"Oh, don't say such things," insisted Grandma.

"Johnathon ... Storms?"

"Oh, you heard about that, huh?"

"Amanda was telling me about it earlier today. Honestly not that long before I came over, actually."

"Amanda's the superstitious type, so she probably didn't tell you what he looked like."

"Quite correct."

"Well, Grandma here's the superstitious type also, so I won't say too much, but if you ever *do* see him—*whew*—he's quite something to behold."

"You've seen him? I mean like, you've actually seen him?"

"Well, glimpses, like I'm sure Amanda told you, but I've been around a lot longer than she has, and I've seen enough of him to put together a rather decent image of him in my head."

"Or so that's what he's telling you," interrupted Grandma.

"I see."

Grandpa laughed. "Oh, this old girl here, always putting me in my place. Or trying to, at least," said Grandpa, winking at Adam.

"Anyway, I'd best be going," said Adam.

"Oh, hey, I think Jacob and Sabrina went to the shops again earlier. Would you mind doing us a favour and making sure they're home before the weather takes a turn for the worse?"

"Not a problem. I'd be happy to. They're great kids."

Grandma shook her head. "What? You can't go out to the store now; the weather could get terribly bad."

"It's quite all right, ma'am. I appreciate your concern, but Amanda too was worried about the kids."

"Yeah, you see. Young, strapping lad like yourself could easily take on Johnathon Storms. Don't even worry about it."

Adam laughed and thanked Grandpa for his encouragement and reassured him that he'd bring back Jacob and Sabrina safely.

"Yeah, you do that." Grandpa smiled. "Okay, off you go now."

Grandpa returned to reading his newspaper, and Adam headed out, keeping in mind to look for Sabrina and Jacob.

A Game of Cricket

Joshua, Jacob and Sabrina were in an older part of the village which contained a no-longer-used, rusted-out old playground, not that far from Grandma and Grandpa's backyard.

"So, where are we going to set up?" asked Joshua, grabbing a nearby garbage bin to use as wickets.

"Hey," called Grandpa from his back porch, "you guys about to play some cricket?"

"Yeah, you gonna come join us?" called Jacob.

"Oh, you bet your britches I am," he replied as he smiled and made his across his backyard to meet them.

"Can I play too?" asked Benji, which startled Grandpa.

"Gah! It's like you come out of nowhere."

"My bedroom window was open, and I heard the three of them talking," said Benji as she pointed towards Joshua, Jacob, and Sabrina. "So, I thought I'd get up, have some breakfast, and see what everyone was up to."

"And you thought it'd be okay to do that in your pyjamas?"

"Sure. Playing cricket's just gonna make me dirty, which means I'm just gonna have to change anyway."

"Wow, I like the way you think."

"Benji!" shouted Sabrina. "Come over and be on our team."

"You're already a team of three, and Grandpa probably needs all the help he can get at his age," she said, a wicked smile across her face.

"Hey! You get yourself over on that team, young lady. I can do just fine by myself."

"And how would you like me on your team?" asked Adam, which made Grandpa jump again.

"Sneaking up on me like, I know who *you've* been spending the most amount of time with recently. Geez."

"Not really sure what you're on about, but sure. I was headed over to the Inconvenience Store but bumped into Angela on her way back from there, and said the kids are probably playing somewhere in the village. Not to mention my ears are finely attuned to the phrase 'a game of cricket,' so here I am."

"Adam!" shouted Jacob. "Come play on our team."

"Um ..." said Adam as he thought about his response with a slight smirk on his face. "Let's make it interesting. Grown-ups versus youngsters."

Joshua's shoulders slumped. He looked at Jacob and Sabrina and started walking towards Adam and Grandpa.

"Hey," said Sabrina, "you're one of us."

At the same time, Adam asked Grandpa why Joshua was approaching them.

"You don't know?"

"It's okay, Grandpa, I heard. I'm in my early twenties, so I guess that makes me an adult, right?"

Adam's eyes widened. "I honestly thought you were a little younger than that. Not much. Around the same age as Belle, I guess."

"Well, if Belle's in her late teens, and I'm in my early twenties, I guess that does make us around the same age."

"Josh," called Sabrina, her shoulders slumped, her jaw agape, and her brow furrowed.

Jacob laughed and assured Josh it was fine.

"What's going on there?" asked Adam.

"They're just really close, that's all," whispered Grandpa.

"You know what, guys?" said Adam. "Just be on whatever team you wanna be on."

"How about," said Amanda, approaching from the around the side of Grandpa's house, "we play people who've been in the village a little longer versus those who haven't been here quite as long." A wide smile spread across her face.

"Well, that's just the two of you and Joshua," said Grandpa as he gestured towards Joshua, "against basically the rest of the village."

"What about," said Angela, having followed Amanda, "we play those who were born in the village versus those who weren't born here. That way, Joshua and Sabrina can play on the same team."

"Yes!" called Sabrina.

"Oh, Mum, that means you're on the same team as me," called Jacob as he waved Angela over.

"Actually, it means I'm on the same team as Adam and Grandpa. I wasn't born in the village. I was born in the city."

"Well, then who does that leave to play on my team?"

"Us," said Max, and he, Julie, Belle, and Donna approached. "We heard people talking, so we thought we'd come find out what was going on."

"Donna's gonna win!" said Donna as she firmly punched her right first into left palm. "Whose team am I on?"

"Mine," said Jacob. "If you were born in the village, you're on my team; if you weren't, you're on the other team."

"So, which team am I on?" asked Belle.

"Ugh," scoffed Donna with a smile. "You can be so absent-minded sometimes, Belle. Go on the other team. You weren't born here."

"She's right," called Angela. "I still remember your mother always says you were born, and I quote, 'in a town far away from here,' so you're definitely on this team," she finished and pointed to the ground.

Sabrina lightly jumped up and down, trying to contain her excitement that she and Joshua would on the same team as she walked from beside Jacob to stand near Joshua, Adam, Grandpa, and the others.

"So, are we all set?" asked Adam.

"Looks like we are," replied Grandpa.

Everyone took their positions and played cricket right up until around morning teatime.

Seeing the Storms

Adam had been around for some time now and still hadn't fully unpacked his things. After a while, a young woman's humming came through the window. He looked out and didn't quite see anyone but definitely heard footsteps getting nearer his house. As he was still unpacking, he caught a glimpse out of his window of a young woman in a white summer dress adorned with a yellow floral pattern, wearing a broad-brimmed straw hat that hid her face. As she hummed a gentle tune, she slowly twirled and danced lightly through the streets. Adam quickly went out to try and introduce himself to her, but before he could get even a few words out of his mouth, it seemed that she had disappeared.

"I wonder who that was?" he said, looking off towards the road that led down to the old, abandoned train station.

"Who?" asked Benji, appearing seemingly out of nowhere.

"Oh!" replied Adam, slightly shocked. "Um, nothing. I just thought a saw a young woman pass by this way. She was humming, and I came out to introduce myself. I thought I'd met everyone already."

Benji asked Adam what she was wearing.

"Oh, that's April Showers. Seeing her is a good omen that the rains are going to be light and gentle this year."

"Oh. When will I get a chance to meet more formally?" replied Adam, Amanda's introduction of the Storms having slipped his mind completely.

Benji giggled. "You just did. She doesn't live here. She only passes through around once every year. You should consider yourself very lucky to have seen her. Not everyone's so lucky."

Adam looked at Benji a little bewildered and confused. "So ..."

"Don't worry about it. It's her cousins, Summer and Johnathon Storms you have to watch out for. Johnathon especially. A big brute of a man, and if you ever see him, pray that you'll survive the storms that he'll bring in his wake."

"That bad, huh?"

"Yeah," said Benji half-heartedly as if hiding a dire truth.

"I'll be sure to let anyone know if I see him."

Clearly feeling uncomfortable, Benji changed the subject and told Adam that Amanda was asking about him earlier and suggested that he should go see her before the day is out.

"You know, just to catch up and stuff. Get to know each other a little better and so on."

"Okay, sure. Hers is the house with the ...?" he said, pointing to where he thought Amanda's house was.

"The one down the end, past the well, near the fountain, two houses before the road that brought you here."

"Oh. Uh," he said, feeling slightly confused. "I think I know which one you mean. I'm sure I'll find it. Thanks."

Riding the Rails

Belle and Amanda had decided to have lunch at the old railway station and looked off to the trees and mountains in the distance. They were sat where one would have sat to wait for the train when it was an active railway, but as Belle finished her yogurt looking down towards the rails, she noticed something peculiar.

"Hey!"

"Huh?" replied Amanda, lost in her own thoughts.

"Those train tracks," she said, pointing. "Those aren't wide enough for full-size train."

Amanda slowly came back to the moment thinking about what Belle had just said, shifting her attention to the narrow-gauge rail. "Hey, you're right."

The two girls looked at each other inquisitively.

"Let's go and ask Grandpa about it," said Belle.

"All right."

Grandpa was dancing whilst doing some housework when he heard a knock at the door.

"Come in," he called out.

It was Belle and Amanda asking about the narrow tracks at the train station.

Grandpa stopped what he was doing for a moment, almost as if happily reminiscent of a time that once was. "Oh, boy, Grandma and I sure did have some wild adventures on that old railroad. Sure, I can laugh about it now, but back then? Oh boy! I'll have to tell you girls about it sometime."

The girls again looked at each other, wondering exactly what kind of adventures Grandma and Grandpa had been on.

"You know what?" said Grandpa, smiling. "I'll tell you guys all about it later, but for now, I want you to do something for me. Go back to the old railway station and follow the tracks to the left towards the grocery store, and you two girls just keep on going until you find a small green shed. Go inside of that shed, and you let me know what you find, okay? I'll probably be in bed by the time you two get back, so tell me tomorrow, but there's plenty of daylight hours left at this time of the year, so head on over, and I'll tell you all about mine and Grandma's adventures tomorrow."

Now back at the old railway station, Belle and Amanda followed the tracks in the general direction of the Inconvenience Store. Amanda voiced her uncertainty to Belle, but Belle just smiled, took Amanda's hand, and pulled her along the tracks.

"Okay, okay, okay, I'm coming, jeez."

"We'll be there in no time, I'm sure of it."

As the two girls walked along, they talked about ordinary things and speculated about the kinds of adventures Grandpa was referring to. Belle asked Amanda about Adam. Amanda asked Belle about Kevin, and eventually they came across a small green shed.

"What do you suppose is in there?" inquired Amanda with a big smile on her face.

"I have no idea," replied Belle.

They once again looked at each other and in unison said, "A train?"

"Let's go find out," said Belle as she hurried towards it.

The shed they'd come to was only just tall enough for a person of reasonable height to fit in. However, it seemed extraordinarily long for something that wasn't unusually wide.

"I like the colour," said Amanda. "It's a nice shade of green."

"How do you open the door?" asked Belle, fingertip glancing against a big, padlocked chain running in front of door.

"We'll just see if it's open, I guess."

Unfortunately for them, the padlock was shut tight.

"Do you suppose there's a key around?" asked Amanda, holding the padlock, looking disappointed.

"Or another way in?" said Belle, noticing a slightly open window on the side of the shed.

The window was open only *just* far enough for Belle to reach her fingers in and push the window open, which, given the age of the shed, was no easy task. "Oh my gosh, Amanda, look. It's a train! It's kind of small for a train, but it's a train, nonetheless. And it's the old-fashioned kind that blows smoke out the top and everything. A steam train," she said, climbing through the window.

"Hey, wait up."

"Go back to the front and I'll see if I can let you in from the inside. Maybe there's a key in here?"

Amanda stuck her head in through the window and was surprised by how bright it was in the shed. Some shelves stood close to the entrance, and she pointed them out to Belle. "See if there's a spare key or something for the padlock over there."

Looking around some more, Amanda realised the brightness was thanks to the strategically located skylights in the roof.

"Found it. I guess it fell out of someone's pocket." said Belle, picking up the key to the padlock. "Hey, go back around to the front. I can probably just slip this under the roller door."

A little annoyed, Amanda went back to the front, and sure enough, Belle slipped the key through which, much to Amanda's surprise, fit the padlock easily and unlocked it effortlessly.

"I don't believe it," she said with a smile on her face.

The chains dropped, she pulled them aside, and Belle opened the roller door from the inside. Now that the main entrance was open, it was much easier to see inside the shed. The train was an old, extremely large-scale model train.

"Do you suppose it's operational?" asked Amanda.

"Well, the way Grandpa was carrying on, it must have worked once upon a time."

"Can you imagine how cramped it would be in one of these tiny little carriages? Even Sabrina's almost as tall."

"Can you imagine how cramped Benji would be in there?"

Belle and Amanda took so long exploring the shed and the train they hadn't realised how much time had gotten away from them and wondered why it seemed so much darker.

"I don't wanna walk home in the dark. What if we get lost?" said Belle in a mild panic.

"It's fine, we'll just follow the rails."

"Eh, it's getting dark, and I'm afraid I might trip."

Suddenly, the train puffed and jutted slightly forwards, startling both Belle and Amanda.

"You don't think," began Belle, "it's trying to tell us something?"

"Well," replied Amanda, "this *is* the train that goes past the shed that houses the vending machine. Maybe they're connected?"

A small red light started flashing inside where the driver would sit. Belle and Amanda briefly stared at each other in stunned silence before Amanda said to Belle, "Get in."

Belle cautiously boarded the carriage closest to the front of the train, and Amanda hopped in and assumed the driver's position.

"*All aboard!*" cried out Amanda, happily, pulling the rope for the train whistle, scaring Belle half out of her wits.

The train started to chug forwards, and Amanda wondered how the headlamp had become active, as she hadn't touched anything herself except for the red blinking button. The train chugged along at a rather leisurely pace, and after a few moments, Belle finally relaxed, enjoying the ride.

"We're here," called Amanda, as the train slowed down to a halt in front of the old railway station.

"Already?"

"Well, it's not like we walked."

"Oh. Right."

Belle and Amanda both got off the train and went the usual way back home, excited about what they'd found and looked forward to telling Grandpa about it tomorrow.

Tomorrow was another day.

When Joshua Arrived

Years before Adam would ever arrive in the village, another stranger made himself known.

Light-grey clouds stretched thinly across the sky, moved by strong wind, accompanied by a light but constantly intermittent rain.

"Mum," called a young Jacob as he looked through the front window and enjoyed the bad weather, "there's a man sitting on our front porch,"

Oh? thought Angela as she looked out the window also, opened it and called out. "Excuse me, can we help you?"

"Do excuse me, ma'am, but I was just passing through when the weather took a turn for the worse, and the closest place to take shelter was here on your porch. I've only been here a moment or two."

As he stood up and turned around, Angela could see that he wasn't a man at all, so much as he was a teenage boy, although he did look mature for his years.

"Oh my, you're just a boy. Please, come in. Make yourself at home." Angela opened the door and held it tight so as not to let the wind get the better of it.

"The name's Joshua. Lost my parents in a train wreck a while back, and no next-of-kin could be found to look after me, so I just thought I'd try and make it my own, wandering from one town to the next, and the next thing I knew I wound up here."

Angela put her hand to her heart as she listened to Joshua's story. "Oh, you must be so lonely."

"I get by."

"You know, there's a small house just a few doors down from here. Feel free to stay as long as you like. I'm sure Grandma and Grandpa wouldn't mind."

"I can stay?" Joshua started to put down his book bag.

"Not, *here* specifically, no," said Angela, her right index finger pointed to the ground "but in the village, certainly. As soon as the weather clears up, we'll take you over."

"That's mighty noble of you, ma'am."

"Oh, please." Angela smiled, shook her head, and waved her hand dismissively in front of her face. "It's the least I could offer."

"We'll, not to be too forward, ma'am, but since you're offering things, I sure wouldn't mind it if you offered me some breakfast. I haven't eaten in days."

"Oh my. Jacob, go upstairs and get Sabrina and have her help you set the table."

"Already done, Mrs. H," called a young Sabrina from the kitchen.

"Oh, Sabrina, you're up already."

"Yeah, I came down the other way."

After breakfast, the weather showed no sign of improvement, so the four of them moved into the living room and decided to play some board games.

"You know what?" said Angela. "You three have fun. I have some housework to do."

"Do you mind if we put the fire on, Mrs. H?" asked Sabrina.

"Yeah, Mum, can we put the fire on?"

"I suppose it is a little chilly today. All right, but just on low, okay?"

Jacob lit the fire, and Jacob, Sabrina, and Joshua all played a wide variety of games, including cards, dice, jacks, marbles, and dominoes.

"So, I guess you'll be staying for a while, huh, Josh?" asked Sabrina.

"We'll see."

Going to the Cinema

It was a cold mid-winter's morning, but the forecast for the rest of the day looked promising. Jacob and Max walked out of their respective front doors to see if anyone else was already up when they noticed each other.

"Hi, Max," called Jacob.

"Hi, Jacob," replied Max. "Julie and I were thinking of going to the old picture theatre later on today and wondered if you and Sabrina would like to join us?"

"Yeah, okay. Is Benji coming too?"

"Maybe. Haven't found out yet. I'll ask her later."

"Yeah, okay then."

Not too far from the village stood an old, unused cinema. In days gone by, its foyer would have been grandiose and spectacular. However, what was once majestic had since given way to the passage of time with the paint peeling of its dank walls and worn-out carpet, long overdue for replacement, the cinema cried out to be renewed. The cinema itself had a ground floor and a balcony and was filled with uncomfortable wooden, leather-cushioned seats. It had the familiar and comforting scent of stained wooden floors. It was an *old* cinema. Max, his sister Julie, and Benji often went there to watch some older films. Being three of the more technically minded teenagers in the village, they'd learned, with some help from Grandpa, how to operate the projection unit and would often go there to keep themselves entertained on some of the more boring days the village had to offer. Rainy days made it an especially popular place to go.

It was later in the day and colder with more snow than what the weather forecast had led everyone to believe, and everyone who was going to be at the cinema was at the cinema. Sabrina and Jacob sat next to each other in two of the seats on the ground floor, talking and being silly, waiting for a movie to be put on. They didn't care and would probably leave before the movie started anyway. They weren't there to watch a movie, they were there to be there.

Out in the foyer, Benji and Julie talked together, while Max went to the projection room and figured out what films to show.

"It's been a while since we put on a show, hasn't it?" said Benji.

"Three weeks isn't that long ago," replied Julie.

"No, I mean an actual show. A performance ... a ... ah, what's the word? An *eisteddfod*, that's it!"

"Oh, *that* kind of a show. Yeah. How long *has* it been?"

"I guess a few months before Adam showed up was our last performance."

"Oh. Not that long ago then, but somehow how longer than I thought."

"I guess as we've gotten older, we've had less and less reason to put on a show, but it'd be fun to do it again some time."

"Maybe at the spring festival."

Max came downstairs from the projection room and told the girls that everything was set up and he just needed one of them to lower the house lights, so Benji went and did that.

Benji and Julie sat in the balcony while Max watched from the projection room. Belle and Donna sat just behind where Sabrina and Jacob were sitting.

The credits came up at the beginning of the film as they so often did back then, and everyone was treated to a story about a girl who was whisked away on a magical adventure. After which, they watched a film about when a young man met a young woman, how they fell in love, how it wasn't meant to be, but all somehow worked itself out in the end.

Sabrina and Jacob left fairly early during the second film, leaving Belle and Donna to sit by themselves for a while.

After the two films were over, everyone who was left gathered in the foyer of the old cinema and, noting the moderate snowfall, decided to stay, make themselves some coffee, and talk about the films they'd just seen. Eventually the talk became a little too girly for Max to handle, so despite the snow, he went home, knowing that'd he'd have nothing constructive to add to the conversation.

As he left, his sister Julie offered him her coat.

"But what about you?" he asked.

"It's fine. I'll just share with Belle. I mean, look at this thing," she said, picking up a part of Belle's winter coat. "It's huge."

"Actually, if it's all the same with you guys," interrupted Benji, "I might go with Max."

After Benji and Max had left, the girls cleaned up after themselves and decided to head home, with Donna following closely behind Belle and Julie.

The wind blew, the snow fell, their hooded fur jackets kept them warm, and they all headed home.

Joshua's Miracle

There hadn't been a gathering of all the townsfolk from the village in one place for quite a while, and the levels of merriment on this Christmas Eve were high.

"Merry Christmas, everyone," said someone in the crowd.

"Merry Christmas," replied a number of people intermittently.

Belle and Sabrina were seated out back, enjoying some of Donna's father's famous cordial. Donna was talking with her father in the kitchen where Jack and Jill and Jacob and Helen were also stirring, taking part in opening Christmas crackers with one another and moaning at the bad jokes that came within them.

Adam and Amanda hadn't yet arrived because, given that they were quite new in their relationship, they always seemed to show up a bit late for most things and leave just a bit early. No one, except for Grandma and Grandpa, (and most of the kids' parents) really knew why.

Joshua hadn't arrived yet either because he was busy tending to the potted plants in his house, which were the single most well-kept potted plants in the entire village. He claimed it was because of the miracle of song, which baffled most people but made perfect sense to Joshua.

"How does singing to his plants give him such a wonderful garden?" people would mutter under their breath in disdain.

Joshua put away his watering can, washed his hands, went inside, and prepared to go to the Christmas party.

"Let's see," said Joshua as he looked through the contents of his fridge, "what do I need to take with me?"

Joshua's fridge was somehow always filled with exactly the right amount of exactly the right contents for whatever the occasion called for. "Hm, I guess I'll just take a crate of wine over. That should satisfy most people, I think."

Back at the Christmas party, Jacob's mother was starting to panic about how low the food and drink supplies were getting and was wondering what do when she remembered she'd overheard someone say that Kevin was planning on heading over to the Inconvenience Store a little later, which, by her reckoning, would be around now.

Scrambling as calmly as possible through the crowd, Jacob's mother looked all around for Kevin and finally noticed Benji, who she knew was quite close with Kevin. "Oh, Benji, there you are. Have you seen Kevin? I was hoping to give him some cash and to ask him to bring back some more food and drink from the store. I heard he was heading that way."

"Oh, he left quite recently. If you like, you can give me the cash, and I'll go and catch up to him. He wouldn't even be as far as the train station by now. Not even close, actually."

"Oh, would you? I'd really appreciate that. I hope this is enough," she said, handing over what seemed to Benji to be a fair sum of money, but what to Jacob's mum seemed a little inadequate.

"We'll do our best to replenish this Christmas party's supplies, ma'am."

"Oh, would you?" said Jacob's mother all too thankfully. "There's no rush, but please hurry," she said as she saw Benji out the door.

"Hi, Missus Holland," called Joshua with a wave and a smile as he noticed Jacob's mother seeing Benji off.

Benji and Missus Holland both acknowledged Joshua.

"Nice to see you finally made it," said Benji, before excusing herself to head off to the store to get some food.

"You've brought some things too, Joshua?"

"Yeah, it's just a crate of old wine I had lying around. Nothing special."

"Oh, great. Here, just put it here on the front porch by the door, and we'll take in a few bottles."

Joshua walked up the front steps of the house, and just before lowering himself down to place the crate, Missus Holland interrupted. "Actually ..."

"Yeah?"

"Around the back might be better. Sorry, Josh."

"No worries, Missus Holland."

Jacob made his way around to the back of the house and up the slightly longer staircase, where he was greeted by Jacob's father.

"Joshua! You made it," said Mister Holland in all too big of a voice. "Here, come put that crate down over here, and we'll be through *all* of that wine by the end of the night, I assure you."

Joshua put down the crate, opened it, took out two bottles, went into the kitchen, and plonked them down on the table in there next to the almost-empty punchbowl and bottles of cordial mix, soda, and various juices. Afterward, he helped himself to some apple juice and started making the rounds, catching up with various people at the party who he hadn't seen in some time.

Benji, being as tall as she was, and walking as fast as she did, was a little surprised she hadn't caught up with Kevin by that point and thought that he must have left earlier than what Missus Holland had thought. It was dark, and Benji didn't like walking to the store by herself in the dark. With friends or family was one thing, but to go all alone made her head spin with all the sorts of things that could happen.

So lost in her thoughts had she become that when the owner of the store called, "Ah, Benji, is it?" she jumped in fright.

"Oh, Mister Jones. You startled me."

"Oh, sorry. I didn't mean to scare you, but someone *that* tall walking *that* fast. Who else could it be?"

Benji smiled and noted that she was there to pick up some extra supplies for the Christmas party at Missus Holland's request, hoping she'd catch up with Kevin on the way.

"Ah, no. Kevin's already been this way, and I believe he went home again. Come in and I'll help you get what you need."

"Thanks, Mr. Jones," said Benji a bit later, receiving the change for the goods she'd just bought for Jacob's mother.

"No worries at all, Benji. I'm just sorry you didn't catch up with Kevin. He's quite the runner."

"Yeah, and knowing him, he'll have gone back home by way of the river. A longer walk, but he seems to enjoy it. I don't much care for going that way in the dark, so I'll just go home the regular way and be comforted by the dim light of the railway station's vending machine."

"Ah. It's like a lighthouse in a storm," began Mister Jones. "You know when you see it that safety and comfort isn't too far away."

"Something like that."

"You stay safe now, and tell Missus Holland and everyone – you know, Jacob, Sabrina, and so on – that I send them my best."

"Okay, Mr. Jones. I'll let them know. Thank you."

"No, thank you."

Benji returned to the village.

Now back at the party, Benji went into the kitchen and unpacked all the contents onto the table.

"Oh, good heavens," said Missus Holland when she saw what Benji had brought back. "You didn't need to get that much!"

"Mr. Jones helped me pack."

"Oh," said Missus Holland with a sigh of relief. "Mr. Jones and his famous Christmas hospitality. Well, that's just the way we'll have to have it then, isn't it?"

"Yes, I guess so."

Meanwhile, for as many people as had been drinking Joshua's generous donation of wine, it just never seemed to run out.

"Three cheers for Joshua and his never-ending crate of red wine! Hip-hip—"

"*Hooray!*" called many merry voices from the crowd.

"Hip-hip—"

"*Hooray!*"

"Hip-hip—"

"*Hooray!*"

They all started singing "For He's a Jolly Good Fellow" and most everyone joined in as the merriment went into the wee hours of the night and long into the next morning.

Merry Christmas, everybody, Merry Christmas.

Playing the Piano

Benji had been learning the piano for a number of years now, and given that it was too cold to do anything outside and most of her friends were otherwise engaged, she decided to try writing an original piece. The kind that she'd heard a lot in movies and on television. However, for all the songs she'd ever listened to, and all the songs she'd ever learnt, she didn't seem to be having much luck. A few notes here and a few notes there, none of which seemed to quite fit together. Being the experienced pianist she was, her seeming lack of ability to write an original song frustrated her immensely. Feeling defeated, she wondered to herself if she'd ever get it right and screamed mildly in anguished frustration.

"Benji, dear, what's wrong?" asked her mother from the living room. "Grandma and I were so enjoying your playing."

Benji got up off the piano stool and walked into the living room where her mother and Grandma were and sat down with them to share in the afternoon tea. "It's just so hard coming up with an original tune. I've never tried it before. I thought it would be easier."

"Oh, it's okay, Benji. What you were playing was just lovely. Maybe it's less so that you're not good at it and more so that you're not yet comfortable with your ability to do it."

Benji never really thought of it like that, and as she contemplated Grandma's words, she thought maybe she'd try again later when she was less frustrated and in a better mood.

"Why don't you try again tomorrow, dear?" asked her mother, echoing her thoughts. "You'll be thinking more clearly after your lunch with Donna."

Grandma giggled. "Always sitting on my front steps, these girls."

"Oh, sorry, I—"

"Oh no, no, it's quite all right, dear, I really don't mind at all. You lot can sit there all you want, okay? We're all family here."

"Thank you, Grandma. I don't know what sort of a song I should write."

"Oh, I see," began Grandma. "Trying to write music from a technical perspective will never do. Music has to come from the heart. Let the spirit of the music move you into so effortlessly playing the keys that you couldn't possibly be enjoying yourself more. Of course, some technicality comes into play, but that comes *after* you've let your emotions dictate to you what you want to play."

"I don't understand."

"Grandma," began Benji's mother, "has a way of over-complicating and unnecessarily romanticizing things. I think what Grandma's really trying to say, Benji, is to play the piano with your heart, not with your head."

Benji looked confused, holding her hands up in front of her she said, "But I play with my hands."

Both Grandma and Benji's mother chuckled as Benji's mother added, "We know, dear. But when writing an original song, you should let your heart, not your head, dictate where your hands should go."

"But I thought ..."

"Let me try again," interrupted Grandma. "Next time you go to the piano, turn off your brain and open your heart."

Hearing Grandma's words, it was like Benji had finally been illuminated in what it meant to not just write, but create an original piece of music, and with that understanding went back to her piano, her frustrations alleviated, and tried again.

Hanging Out the Laundry

It was an ordinary day, as ordinary as any the village had ever experienced, and no one was complaining. Children played in the streets, adults sat on the front porches of their houses, and Amanda was at home, doing her laundry.

Looks like I'm gonna have to go to the store later and get some more powder, Amanda thought, picking up the almost empty box of powder and pouring it into the washing machine.

"Hey, Adam," she lightly called out, as she walked out to the back of the house where her clothesline was. She waited there for the washing machine to finish.

"Yeah?" he replied.

"Have the kids taught you their pet name for the grocery store?"

"Oh, ah," began Adam, staring up at the clouds, as he watched them drift by, "the Inconvenience Store. Why's that?"

"Just ... wondered. But do you know *why* they call it that?"

"Because it's so inconvenient for them to have to walk that far to get some groceries."

"Wow, you're really fitting in around here, huh?" said Amanda, smiling.

"Thanks. I'm trying my best. As for Inconvenience Store, I don't see why they don't just get a bike. And it's a pity that billycart fell apart on them. It's probably quite fixable."

"Don't mention a bike to the kids," said Amanda in slight shock.

"What happened?" replied Adam, propping himself up on his elbows.

Amanda lowered her head and tried to say nothing but gave in, asking Adam to come up to the porch so she could tell him over a glass of cordial.

"Grandpa's famous cordial?" he said in excitement, getting up, brushing himself off, and hurrying up to the porch.

"I think you mean Donna's father's famous cordial."

"Right."

Amanda returned with two glasses of red cordial and told Adam a woeful tale of how a small group of young children, nervous about having stolen a bike they knew they weren't supposed to ride, ended up killing an innocent animal one day on the way back from the Inconvenience Store.

"Oh ... what happened next?"

Amanda continued to tell the tale of how those children, attempting to right their wrongs, gave the animal an honourable burial and discarded the bike somewhere down by the river. "When some of the older kids and I went to gather the bike, it seemed that another small animal had somehow got caught up in it and as Angela and I tried to free it, something happened, and Angela's fingers broke."

"Holy God, they just snapped right off or what?"

"Adam, please, take this seriously."

"I am. I'm just ... trying to understand."

"Angela and I never got on too well, and she had hopes of being a concert pianist one day, so when her fingers broke, she blamed it on me, and we've not had the best of relationships ever since."

"Amanda, I don't know what to say."

"And it was mine."

"Sorry?"

"The bike. The one the kids weren't supposed to ride. It was mine. I guess it still is. It's propped up somewhere by the old railway station, I think."

"Wow, that's a lot to take in," said Adam before continuing to sit there in a sort of stunned silence, thinking about everything he'd just heard.

The washing machine rattled to a stop as that cycle of the washing finished.

"I should hang out the laundry."

"Okay then."

Walking with Intent

Joshua's clothing was similar to what Adam had worn on his first day in the village, and thinking back on all of his years in the village with a warm sense of nostalgia, he now knew he was ready to take on whatever life was willing to throw at him.

"Joshua!" called Sabrina, running as fast as her feet could carry her. "Josh, wait!" she cried out with a strong sense of yearning. "Where are you going? And why?"

Joshua turned around as he heard Sabrina's all-too-familiar footsteps running towards him, and he smiled and reached out his arms for a hug. Tears streamed down her face as she hugged him back.

"You're like the closest thing to an older brother I've got. I know you're not really my brother, but sometimes it really feels like it, you know?" she said, sobbing heavily.

"I was hoping no one would tell you."

"They didn't. I went over to your place this morning, and it was all packed up *way* too nice, and was *way* too clean for something not to be going on. I remembered years ago when you told me that when the day came that I entered your house and you weren't there and it looked more immaculate than a brand-new hotel room, that would be the day you would leave the village for good, so I came running. I didn't want you to leave without me saying goodbye. Why are you leaving anyway? *Why?*"

"Because of things that only I can do. Things that I have to do."

"But what if when you come back, you're not the same person I'm saying goodbye to now?"

"If when I come back, I'm still the same person I am now, then I've probably not learned the life lessons I was supposed to. I assure you, Sabrina, if I change at all, it'll be for the better."

"I *hate* change. Change always means losing something."

"Sabrina, change doesn't mean losing anything. It just means something's changed. And besides, Adam's arrival was a *big* change, and there most certainly wasn't any kind of a loss then, was there? If anything, it was a gain."

"Oh," said Sabrina, wiping tears from her eyes, having settled down somewhat, "I never thought of it like that."

"Can I join you? At least part of the way?"

"Me too!" added Jacob, who had apparently turned up out of nowhere.

"You have to understand that I'm going *so* much further away than the Inconvenience Store. That isn't even a tenth of how far I'm going to travel, not even a hundredth. I'm going to a place that's far beyond where the horizon lies."

"Jacob and I can *easily* walk that far."

"Even with my bad knee, I could walk that far. I'd even dare myself to walk twice as far!"

"Sabrina, Jacob. Believe me, I understand why you want to come with me, but you need to understand that you can't. What would the village do without the two of you? How badly would Grandma and Grandpa miss you? And what of Adam and Amanda? What would the two of them do without the two of you? Not to mention Kevin."

"But what if I asked you those same things?"

"Ah, clever girl. I've already made my peace with Grandma and Grandpa about leaving, and perhaps Adam understands better than anyone why I have to leave, but I assure you, Sabrina, all of your friends, old and new, are going to take excellent care of you, and you them. So please, let me do what I have to do."

"Please, can we come with you? At least as far as the train station?"

"All right then, to the train station."

"Okay," agreed Sabrina and Jacob.

Around twenty minutes later, the three of them arrived at the train station, where Joshua decided to stop in and get a drink from the vending machine.

"Sabrina recommends the apple juice," said Jacob, pointing out the apple juice through the glass screen of the vending machine, "but I prefer the soda."

"Hm ..." said Joshua contemplatively. "I wonder if that old tap is still outside."

"I think it's broken," replied Jacob.

The three of them went outside to check, and as Jacob tried to turn it, it appeared to be rusted stiff. "Yeah. Broken."

To the sheer and utter amazement of both Sabrina and Jacob, when Joshua knelt down to turn the tap, he turned it as effortlessly as the day it was installed.

"Excellent," he said, holding an empty flask under it, waiting for the water to come.

"But won't the water be dirty?" asked Sabrina.

A moment later, the pipes of the tap rattled and banged, as water hadn't been through them in decades, and much to Sabrina's surprise and Jacob's confused curiosity, the water was as clean and as clear as the sky was blue.

"This tap should be fine for you guys to use from now on."

"Really?"

"Really. Okay, guys, this is where I leave ... and you stay."

Jacob and Sabrina sat on an old bench outside the train station as they watched Joshua walk down the road towards the Inconvenience Store and were happy to see that he turned back every now and again with a wave and a smile. He eventually disappeared around the bend of the road, no longer to be seen.

"We should go back home now," said Sabrina.

"But I wanna follow him some more."

"He asked us not to follow him further than the train station, and we should respect his wishes."

"All right then. Let's go home."

Visiting Kevin
and Sitting by the River

Winter had long since gone, and it was finally a nice enough day to wear loose-fit clothing and shorter sleeves. It was just past morning teatime, so Belle and Donna, Sabrina and Benji had all decided to go for a walk to the next town over to see what Kevin was up to.

Today, rather than go by the old train station, they'd decided to go by the river to better enjoy the sunshine, noting that the shade of the trees in the other direction may have made the temperature cooler than desirable.

"Jacob's not with you, Sabrina?" asked Belle.

"Not today. Angela said his violin practice has been slipping lately, so she's making him stay home all day to practice."

"All day?" asked Donna in shock.

"Angela's just liked that sometimes." Sabrina shrugged.

"I actually really like Angela, but she sure can be strict sometimes," said Belle, stretching her arms as she walked.

"I'm so glad my parents are relatively easy-going." Benji smiled.

Donna scoffed. "Well, we can't all be as lucky as you now, can we?"

Benji laughed.

"I hope Kevin likes the tea I served him last time," said Belle with a raised eyebrow, a smile stuck on her face.

Donna stopped dead in her tracks, choked on words she wanted to say but couldn't.

"What's wrong?" asked Sabrina, a little worried.

"Belle, you've ..." began Donna, trying to process what she'd just heard, still a little lost in the thoughts of what she just heard. "You've served Kevin tea?"

"Yeah, so?"

"But *I've* served Kevin tea."

"Hm," said Benji. "It seems Kevin is not a single-minded man."

"So what if you both served Kevin tea? It's just a drink," interrupted Sabrina.

Benji and Belle looked at each other and laughed.

"Is there something I'm not getting here?" asked Sabrina.

"It's nothing. Don't worry about it," said Donna in a huff. "I'm going back to the village."

"Oh, I'll go with you," said Sabrina, having not really wanted to go to the next town over in the first place.

"Okay," said both Belle and Benji. "We'll see you when we come home this evening."

"Yeah, whatever," said Donna, already walking away.

"Oh, and we'll tell you all about our dancing lessons with Kevin," added Benji, both she and Belle still smiling and laughing.

A park bench situated by the side of the river had on it a metal plaque which read "In Loving Memory Of", but the name of who it was in loving memory of had faded over time, so no one really knew who it was the bench was honouring.

Donna sat down on the bench, placed her elbows on her knees and her face into her fists. Sabrina sat down next to her and asked her if it was something she wanted to talk about.

"Not really," replied Donna. She sighed and said, "I just thought Kevin and I ... Kevin and me ... whatever the correct term is. I mean, like, so ... he and Belle ... Belle and I ... Kevin. Oh, I don't know," she finished, her arms now folded.

"Well, it seems to me like—oh, do you want a soda pop?" asked Sabrina, as she handed Donna the drink.

"It seems to you like wh— Where did you get this? *When* did you get this?"

"It seems to *me* like you're unwilling to admit that you've got feelings for Kevin."

"Oh," she said as she moved her gaze to the river. "I guess that could be true."

"And I got these from the vending machine at the abandoned train station."

"We didn't go to the old train station."

"*You* didn't go to the old train station. I went right before we left and caught up with you guys right after."

"But you were with us the whole time."

"No, I caught up with you. You do realise the train station's just over there, right," she said, pointing behind the bench and through the trees.

Donna looked behind her, her mouth agape, an eyebrow raised. "Sometimes the layout of this place confuses the daylights out of me."

"I try not to think about it. Do you wanna forget all about Kevin and go for a walk to the department store?"

"Kevin? You mean—oh! Actually, I'd already forgotten, and you mean the Inconvenience Store, right?"

"Nope. I mean the department store. The big one in the city."

Wide eyed and expressionless, Donna looked so directly into Sabrina's eyes; it was as if she were piercing her heart and soul with merely a look.

"What?" said Sabrina, slightly taken aback.

"Haven't you ever noticed the trees at the end of the dark forest before you board the ferry to cross the river to the city arch over in such a way that it looks like an open book? A big, ominous, intimidating open book."

"Actually, I haven't," Sabrina replied, paused in thought, trying to remember what the opening at the end of the dark forest looks like.

"And at just the right time of day," continued Donna, "if the light casts shadows in just the right way, and a flock of birds fly from one side to the other, or perhaps some leaves carried on a breeze, it looks as if the pages are turning."

Sabrina stared blankly at Donna for a moment, a smile forming on her face, clearly trying to prevent a laugh, but it couldn't be helped, and Sabrina laughed.

Donna shuddered. "It's not funny! It gives me the creeps every time."

"Sorry," said Sabrina, trying not to laugh, "but I didn't realise you were so imaginative."

"Seeing the edge of the dark forest like that makes me feel like when I'm in the village I'm comfortably snuggled into the pages of an easy-to-read book, but on the other side, it's like—how do I put this?—It's like I'm in the wrong book."

Sabrina opened her eyes wide, smiled, and slowly nodded.

The conversation continued, the day slowly marched on, and after a while Sabrina asked Donna if she wanted to go back to the village, and they did.

Messing Up the Hall

The afternoon had firmly set in with the twinkling stars of twilight slowly introducing themselves as the evening sky became ever darker.

Jacob and Sabrina, Belle and Donna, Julie and Max, and Kevin and Benji were all helping decorate the Town Dinner Hall in preparation of the spring festival, somewhat unimaginatively titled *The Spring Festival*, forever held around this time of year, but never on a specific date.

Jacob and Sabrina stood on a sturdy plank held up by two ladders in a manner that reminded them both of having painted the wall when Adam first arrived. They were hanging up one of many paper chains along the walls.

"I'm still a little worried about that storm we saw on the horizon on that way back from the shops yesterday," said Jacob as the wind picked up outside, rattling the doors.

"You mean the Inconvenience Store?"

"Yes, I mean the stupidly faraway Inconvenience Store!"

"Hence, why I said Inconv—"

"Stop saying 'hence' all the time," demanded Jacob.

Sabrina replied with a stunned silence and paused for a moment before returning to hanging up the decorations, whispering to herself, "Just because other people my age aren't well read doesn't mean I shouldn't be."

"Oh, sorry, Sabrina. It's just that my sore knee gets to me sometimes and makes me cranky."

"No, it's okay, Jacob. You don't have to make up excuses. Let's just get back to putting up these decorations. It's awkward with Benji watching us."

"Hey!" called Benji from across the room. "I heard that. I heard your little spat too."

"Sorry," called Sabrina.

"Don't you think it's weird," began Benji, "how sometimes people who seem like the best of friends can lose a lifelong friendship over the smallest of things?"

"Who are you talking to?" called Jacob as he continued about his business.

"Kevin, if you don't mind."

"Not at all. Sorry."

As Benji sat on the steps that led up to the stage at the front of the hall, she waited for a reply, but as she looked around, she noticed that Kevin had gone somewhere, leaving behind his wallet.

Why leave just your wallet behind? she thought, picking up the wallet, looking at it curiously before putting it back down and continuing with her paper-chain making.

"Oi," she said, calling out to Belle and Donna, who were busy deciding the best place for the placement of tables and chairs. "Did either you see where Kevin went?"

Belle and Donna looked at each other, seeing if the other person knew where Kevin had gone, both sharing with each other a blank facial expression implying that not only did they not know, but wondering why Benji thought either of them *would* know.

"Actually," began Donna, "neither of us has a clue. But I heard what you were saying before, and I noticed their little spat too. And honestly? I wouldn't worry about it. Belle and I used to have little spats like that all the time. In some ways, it can help make the friendship stronger. Next time he won't be so direct, and he'll likely try and do a better job at explaining himself. At least hopefully he will, anyway."

"Then why didn't he just do it like that in the first place?"

"Ah, a-ha. Because he probably didn't know he was supposed to, and what he said probably didn't sound like something mean to say until he heard himself say it out loud."

"Wow. I guess some people are really stupid, huh?" said Benji.

"I heard that!" came a cry from across the room, which in turn caused Sabrina to cup her hands over her mouth in an attempt to stop herself from laughing.

"Hey!" said Jacob, spinning around to face Sabrina. "What are *you* laughing at?"

"Nothing," she said, failing miserably at trying not to laugh.

Jacob climbed down from the ladder and stormed out to the front of the hall, where he sat on the front steps and sulked.

"Ah, Jacob," called Benji as she watched Jacob storm off. "I'm really sorry. I didn't mean to upset you. I just need to learn to put my brain in gear before I let words come out of my mouth. Sorry, okay?"

"Sounds like something you both need to learn," said Belle under her breath.

"Excuse me, Belle, what?"

"Oh, nothing. Just mumbling to myself," replied Belle sheepishly.

"Don't worry about it," interrupted Donna as she sorted out where the Styrofoam cups would go. "He'll be over it by tomorrow."

"Ah, I really should learn to think before I speak, and besides," she said, lowering her voice, "I didn't think he could actually hear me from all the way over there."

"Actually," began Donna, "sound travels really well in this building."

"Not to be rude, Ben, but maybe you should just go look for Kevin?"

"Ah, good idea. I've finished this paper chain for now, anyway."

Benji picked up Kevin's wallet, walked up the stairs onto the stage, and made her way around to the back of the stage using the same exit that she believed Kevin would have used to leave.

Benji's long, dark brown hair was being blown all over the place because of the ever-increasing wind, sometimes so badly that her hair was actually horizontal.

"Kevin?" she called out, walking away from the back of the hall, but trying not to stray too far.

She put his wallet in her top-left, inside jacket pocket, knowing it would be safe there.

"Kevin!" she called again as loud as she could, looking for signs of his whereabouts.

When she realised his shoe prints went off in the direction of the Inconvenience Store, she became incredibly worried. A whirlwind of questions started flurrying through her mind, such as if she should tell anyone and if she did, who should she tell? She wondered if she should go and tell her parents or if she should she go back into the hall and tell the other kids. *Do Kevin's own parents even know where he's gone?*

And with that last question she paused for a moment and thought, *Wait. Does Kevin even* have *parents?*

"Grandma will know what to do," she said.

Fighting the wind, Benji made her way to Grandma's house which, even though it was only seven houses away, the wind made it seem more like ten miles.

By the time Benji had arrived at Mr. and Mrs. G's house, a constant rain had started falling.

"Good heavens, dear," said Grandma as she opened the door to let Benji in, "what on Earth are you doing out when the weather's like this?"

"A few of us kids were over at the Town Dinner Hall preparing for the Spring Festival when the weather turned bad, and I suddenly realised Kevin wasn't there anymore. I didn't know who I should tell, so I came here."

"Oh, don't worry about Kevin, dear."

"Yeah," called Grandpa, "Kevin can look after himself."

"But—"

"I wouldn't worry about it. He's probably down at the grocery store by now, anyway. At the very least taking cover in that rickety old train station."

"Yeah," began Benji, "it's the rickety part that worries me."

"No. That old train station is as sturdy now as the day it was built."

"Thanks for trying to make me feel better, Grandpa, but I seriously doubt that."

"You kids have no faith in old technology these days."

"Anyway, I should get back to the others."

"No!" called both Mr. and Mrs. G in unison.

"You stay here, dear," said Grandma. "The weather's getting far too bad at this point. Best you just stay and have some of my cookies."

"Thanks, Grandma," said Benji, sitting down in the living room taking one of Grandma's cookies.

Surviving the Storms
and Cleaning Up the Village

The following morning's weather was so pleasant, it was almost as if the previous night's storm hadn't happened at all, although the wreckage in the village suggested otherwise. Potted plants were overturned, dirt spilled out everywhere, some far from their owners' houses. Branches of trees on people's houses, or in worse cases, through their windows. Occasionally a dead rat could be seen here or there.

Belle woke up first, looking around, wondering where she was as she slowly realised that she and the others had spent the night at the Town Dinner Hall because of the bad weather.

"Is everyone all right?" she asked.

She looked around, and as the others heard her voice, they started to stir.

Julie woke up next. "Is who all right? Who's everyone? Where are we? Oh, the hall."

She and Belle both glanced at each other, then they looked around the hall, realising that, thankfully, everything was still basically as it was the night before.

"Should we wake the others and keep going with the preparations?" asked Julie.

Belle looked back and forth amongst the others and around the room. "I think it'd be best if we just start working, and the noise of our commotion will wake up the others eventually anyway."

"Understood."

They both got up, and as they moved the tables around, Belle caught a glimpse outside. "Julie, come look at this."

"Why, what is it?" Julie walked over to see what Belle was focused on and couldn't believe her eyes. "Oh."

Wide eyed, they grabbed each other's hands in a slight panic.

"Benji!" they both said.

"What is it?" replied Benji, as if appearing from nowhere, accidentally scaring both Julie and Belle.

"Ah!" they jumped in fright.

"How do you *do* that?" asked Belle.

"Yeah," added Julie.

"Do what?" asked Benji, genuinely curious about what she meant.

"Show up out of *nowhere* as if you were right there the *whole time*?"

"It's almost as if you can teleport."

"Eh? Teleport? You mean just click my fingers and stop being in one place and start being in completely different place, just like that," she said, smiling as clicked her fingers.

"Exactly," said Julie and Belle in unison.

"Actually, I can," she said, readying her fingers to click; her beaming smile stuck across her face.

An expression of surprised confusion crossed both Belle and Julie's faces.

"Just watch." She clicked her fingers and jumped sideways from where she was standing. "See? I clicked my fingers, and suddenly stopped being where I was and am now where I wasn't."

Belle slapped her forehead and rolled her eyes, while Julie couldn't stop laughing.

It was around ten o'clock now, and Grandpa, after having cleaned up around his house, was ready to tackle the village at large.

"All right, let's see what the damage is," he said as he walked out his front door, surprised it wasn't nearly as bad as what he remembered from when he first looked before cleaning up his own place.

"Adam?" he called out as he saw Adam and Amanda helping clean the village.

"Oh, Grandpa. Hi. Amanda and I thought we'd help out. Looking around, I'd say we're *mostly* finished but won't be *completely* finished until around midday."

"Huh," said Grandpa, his mouth agape, his eyes wide with stunned confusion. "How'd you manage to get so much cleaned up in so little time?"

"It's how I was brought up, and it's who I am. And it's who I am *because* of how I was brought up. You and all the people here have welcomed me into this village as one of your own, and I thought helping cleaning up after such a big storm would be the least I could do. Not to mention Amanda here's been a big help. Couldn't've done it in twice the time if it wasn't for her."

"Hi, Grandpa." Amanda waved.

"Say, when you kids are done here, would you mind running down to the store, checking on old man Jones, and clearing up any mess at the old train station on your way back?"

"Done and done. Mr. and Mrs. Jones are fine, and they send their regards."

"You mean to tell me that you've not only checked in on the Joneses at the store down the road, cleaned up the old train station on your way back, but *also* cleaned up *most* of the damage from last night's storm?"

"He's been up since the crack of dawn," said Amanda. "I wasn't sleeping well and didn't have anything better to do, so I thought I'd join him."

"Who *are* you, Adam? Superman?"

Later in the day, with a little help from everyone, the town had been completely cleaned up, and people were gathered in the town square, enjoying an early-afternoon tea, children playing in the streets.

Angela was discussing with Grandpa how thankful she was that the storm was over and everyone was safe. "I don't know what I'd do if anything ever happened to my little Jacob."

"That storm was a doozy, that's for sure, and there's definitely been worse in years gone by, but you're right to be glad that it's passed."

"Given how bad *that* storm was, I really don't think we'll be seeing another one of *those* for quite some time."

"Well, you never can tell, dear," he said, his eyes fearfully lingering on a distant horizon. "You never can tell."

Splashing in and by the River

It was another nice day, and a few people had decided to go and have a picnic by the riverside. Angela and Amanda set up the one and only picnic table on this side of the river. Jacob and Sabrina were on the grass playing some style of ring-toss game. Benji, Julie, and Max were playing games involving skipping ropes, rocks, and elastic, but no one seemed to be quite sure what they were playing, including themselves. Belle and Donna were having fun splashing around in the river, competing with each other about how capable they were as swimmers, and other tricks that could done only in water.

Amanda and Angela sat next to each other, facing the river. That way they could keep an eye on Belle and Donna together.

"Thank God that storm's over," said Angela with a smile and a breath of relief.

"Yeah," replied Amanda. "If previous years are anything to go by, that's the worst of it for this year."

"Exactly. We can just forget all about it and get on with our lives. Johnathon Storms has been and gone."

"I wonder who saw him this year."

"Wonder who saw who this year?" interrupted Benji, having finished playing with Julie and Max.

"You really *do* show up as if out of nowhere, don't you, Benji?" Angela pointed out.

"Not really," began Amanda. "I mean, she was just over there playing the whole time. It's not like we didn't know where she was or anything."

"Right," said Benji. "I think people just get so lost in their own thoughts, they don't realise I've shown up."

"Anyway," said Angela, "we were just wondering who—if anyone—saw Johnathan Storms this year."

Benji paused as she thought for a moment. "Well, Adam saw April Showers."

"Well. That was definitely a *storm*. Not a *shower*. Unless ..."

"Unless what?" said Grandpa, placing down a picnic basket on the table.

"Oh! Grandpa." Angela jumped. "Jeez, first Benji, now you. Where's Mum?"

"Dear old Grandma is right there playing ring-toss with Jacob and Sabrina."

"Wait," said Amanda, "Grandpa is your dad?"

"Well, it's not like I was hiding it. I just never specifically said it."

Benji added that she thought everyone knew, looking at Amanda curiously. "How long have you been here again, Amanda?"

Amanda laughed off Benji's comment, only to realise that she couldn't actually remember. "That's a good question, actually. How long *have* I been here?"

"Anyway," said Angela, "we were just talking about the recent storm, and Benji said that Adam saw April Showers this year, but I was thinking what if it wasn't April Showers at all, but Summer Storms."

"You know," began Grandpa, "sometimes bad weather is just bad weather."

In the river, Belle and Donna were splashing around, having fun, swimming against the current of the river at that one point where everyone knew the current was just a little stronger for some reason, seeing who could last the longest. As they'd grown older, they always wondered who'd get tall enough first to just simply be able to walk across the river, but even for Benji, it got too deep, although she was easily the person who could make it the furthest across the river before having to tread water, Belle coming in a close second. As for Donna, well, even Sabrina was starting to be able to walk further across the river than Donna before having to tread water.

"You might be able to walk further across the river than I can, Belle, but I'll always be a stronger swimmer," called Donna, staying firmly in place against the river's current.

Belle smiled. "You know I sometimes swim to the next town over to meet Kevin, right?"

"Really?" replied Donna in confused awe.

"Really."

"Ugh." Donna rolled her eyes. "Then there's no way I'm a stronger swimmer than you. Then again, how could I stay here against the current like this if I'm *not* a stronger swimmer than you?" She smiled.

"You know I know you've got your foot propped up against that log that's been there forever, right?"

"Forever?" inquired Donna with a smile.

"Well, you know, since we put it there when we were kids."

"Since we were kids? It wasn't *that* long ago. Only a few years."

"Then I guess we see things differently."

"Ah, yeah, I guess. Actually, I've been here so long I think I might be a bit stuck."

"Oh, you mean like you were 'stuck' last time?"

"What?" said Donna, a smile ten miles wide across her face.

"You know *exactly* what! I'm not falling for that again."

"No, I don't know, really. Remind me." An impossibly wide smile stuck across Donna's face.

"It's not funny. You tricked me into thinking you were stuck, and when I was down there trying to free your feet, I thought you were leaning on me for support, but you took my top off!"

"You mean *this* top?" said Donna, lifting Belle's top up out of the river on her fingers.

Belle ducked lower into the river, not that it mattered, as the river wasn't that clear in the first place—nor was it particularly unclear—it just wasn't clear either. Her face became extremely flush.

"When did you even do that? Give it back!" said Belle, trying not to make a fuss or a scene.

"The real question is how did you not even notice until just now?"

Belle replayed the entire morning's events back in her mind, trying to figure out exactly where and when Donna would've had a chance to have taken her top from her.

"I can't think of when you would've had ample opportunity. When *did* you take it?"

"Actually," began Donna, now more sombre than before, "truth be told, I didn't take it all. Not in my usual sneaky way at least. Not intentionally."

Donna explained to Belle that it was when they were competing with each other against the current of the river, and she saw her strap coming undone. "In fact, you're lucky."

"I am?"

"It was just as we'd agreed to stop competing. It slipped off just as you ducked under the water and moved to where you are now. You're lucky I noticed and caught it before it floated off down the river, otherwise it'd be more than halfway to the next town over by now."

"Give it back," said Belle calmly.

"Okay. Come over here and let me help you put it back on. I mean, I *am* stuck here, but like, stuck on purpose. Secured! That's the word I'm after. I'm secured in position over here."

Belle moved over to Donna and allowed to her to put her top back on when Donna suddenly asked Belle about Adam. Belle's face again became flush, and her demeanour unexpectedly coy.

"Oh my God, you like Adam."

"Can you keep a secret?"

"You know I can, Belle. Sure, I might have a loud and boisterous personality, but you *know* I can keep a secret. I even know how long Amanda's been here."

Belle looked over towards Amanda and wondered why Donna would even say such a thing.

"In fact, I'm probably the best secret-keeper in the entire village."

Belle, her top now securely fastened, turned and looked curiously at Donna, taking in what she'd just said. "So ... do you know who stocks the vending machine?"

"You know what? We're closer to this riverbank, and I think we're both starting to shiver. Let's get out here."

Belle agreed, and once they'd climbed out, Donna happily shouted across the river to the others not to worry about them and they'd make their way back to the village in their own time. They sat across from each other at one of the few picnic tables on this side of the river. This one had a canopy.

"You wanted to tell me something about Adam?"

"Well, yeah, I'll tell you about Adam, but *do* you know who stocks the vending machine?"

"Ugh, fine. I figured if anyone would know, it'd be Grandpa, so I've asked him a few times, but he just laughs it off, gives me some vague answer, and subtly changes the subject. So, to answer your question, no, I don't know who stocks the vending machine. Although to tell you the truth, I'm starting to wonder if it just stocks itself."

"Huh," said Belle as she pondered the same thing, then smiled at the thought. "Don't be silly. Someone from *somewhere* has to stock it, right? I guess it's probably just Mr. Jones from the store."

"It could be, but honey, we've gone off topic. You were going to tell me about Adam?" she said with a smirk and a briefly raised eyebrow.

"The night Adam first came to town, I couldn't sleep, and I noticed Adam's lights were on, so I decided to go and make him some tea."

Donna's eyes lit up. "You mean the same tea you give to Kevin?"

"The very same. And we danced together too."

"You served him tea *and* you danced with him?"

"Well, we had to do *something* while we waited for the kettle to boil, right?"

Donna looked over her shoulder, back towards the other side of the river, specifically looking at Amanda. "I wouldn't worry about it."

"Worry about what?"

"Adam and Amanda seem perfectly smitten with each other, and it was his first night here, so it was before they met."

Belle smirked, raised an eyebrow, and told Donna, "You know I'm not the sort of girl to worry about something like that."

"Then what's the problem?"

Before Belle had a chance to answer, a rather sudden an unexpected downpour began to fall.

"What in the world?" said Donna.

"Where did *this* come from?" asked Belle.

Both girls looked across the river in a panic and saw the others hurriedly packing up, Grandpa calling out to them and using strong gestures to suggest they stay on that side of the river and make their way back home by following the tracks to the train station. The same train station where Adam arrived all those months ago.

"That would take forever," said Donna. "It'd be quicker to swim back across."

"No," said Belle suddenly. "Grandpa's right. The canopy of the trees is pretty thick over here, so it might protect us from the rain better."

"But what if a train comes along?"

"We'll flag it down and hitch a ride. They don't travel that fast around these parts, anyway. And besides, how often do trains even come this way?"

"Well, can't we follow it that way to the next town over?"

"No. We're on the opposite side of the river, and the train tracks go some other place, far, *far* away from the next town over. The next stop's even further away than the city and in completely the opposite direction."

"Belle, I *really* think we'd be better off risking swimming across. It's not like we haven't swam in the river with rain heavier than this before," she said, her hand out to feel the rain, her eyes sky-bound to assess the severity of the weather.

"I dunno, Donna. Something's not right. Something just feels ... off, you know?"

"Look," said Donna as she pointed to clouds swiftly gathering above the village. "That face in the clouds. You can barely make it out, but it's definitely there."

"Face? What are you talking about?" asked Belle as she looked up. Her eyes widened in shock. "Johnathon."

Belle and Donna looked at each other in shock. "You're right, Donna. We have to get home as quickly as possible. You think you can make it?"

The river was acting strangely, not just with the pitter-patter of the heavy rains, but there were passing swells in the direction of the next town over.

"I'm willing to try. What's the worst that could happen, anyway? We'll just end up swept down to the next town over, right?"

"Now's not the time to make light of this."

"Ready when you are."

They both hopped back into the river and started to make their way across, the current unexpectedly pulling and tugging at them every which way you could imagine. After not too long, Donna thought that maybe Grandpa was right and searched for Belle to tell her they should go back, but she couldn't see her anywhere.

"Belle?" she called out.

Suddenly, the river was wider than it had ever been in her life, and she seemed to be in about the middle of it. Gazing over to the main tracks, and back again towards the village side of the river, she was shocked when she saw a landslide fall into the river, taking quite a few trees with it. "There's no going back that way now."

She continued with all her might to swim across to the village side of the river.

As Belle got in the river with Donna, she decided to dive under the water, thinking the current wouldn't pull her around as much down there as it did on the surface, but as she lowered herself, she was swept away in the direction of the train station. When she finally came up for air, she was shocked at how far she'd been taken. "Donna?" she called out.

In the distance, Belle heard what sounded like the creaking of falling trees, knowing that could only mean one thing. "Landslide," she said. "There's no way Donna could make it up this way now. I'll just hope that she's as strong a swimmer as she brags she is." She climbed up onto the riverbank and made her way to the train station.

"Belle!" shouted a familiar male voice. "Belle. Over here. It's Grandpa."

Grandpa, waving a lantern in the air, saw that Belle had heard her name, and he stood there patiently as he watched her hurry in the direction of his voice.

"Grandpa. You have no idea how relieved I am to see you. To see anyone."

"Where's Donna?"

"There was a landslide."

"A landslide? And Donna?" His heart sank.

"Wait," said Belle as her thoughts raced around from one possibility to another. She frantically looked around and realised that Donna was nowhere to be seen. "When I started swimming, I thought she wasn't that far behind me, but the landslide—she must've—I mean, she—I thought that—"

"You know what?" said Grandpa to distract Belle back to the present moment. "Here are your clothes and a towel," he said, handing her a satchel. "There's a shower in the amenities area of this station. Why don't you go wash yourself off, get freshened up and tell me all about it on the way back in the car."

"What's a car?" she asked, trying to see out the front of the station as she caught a glimpse of it. "Oh! A horseless carriage," said Belle, happily surprised as she made her way to the showers. "I didn't know you had one of those, Grandpa."

"Well, I guess I'm just full of surprises. Now go change. I'll be right here."

"Right."

Johnathon

L ater that day, the weather was slowly getting worse, and Benji, Julie, Max, Amanda, and Angela had all gathered in the Town Dinner Hall after coming back from the picnic by the river. At first, they'd hoped to stay there until the weather lightened up a little bit and each go back to their respective homes, but as the as time passed, the weather only worsened.

"What's that sound?" asked Angela, hearing a strong and constant thudding sound coming from outside.

"It sounds like," began Julie, focusing carefully on the sound, "footsteps."

"Look," said Angela. "Who is that?"

Benji, Julie, and Max all gathered beside Angela to look out the window and were shocked by what they saw.

A strong *thud* accompanied each one of the slow, deliberate footsteps, one after another. Julie, Max, and Amanda each noticed separate things about Johnathan: his leather boots with belt-like straps; his thick, heavy, dark-grey trench coat, drenched from the rain; and finally his fingerless black leather gloves, covering his strong hands.

"Should we let him in?" asked Julie.

"Not if that's who I think it is," said Angela, just as the front doors opened with a creak. "No." She turned to see that Max and Benji had gone to let him in. "*No!* Get back here you two, *now*!" she said as she ran to catch up with them, but it was already too late, as they were both outside, and the door somehow refused to open for Angela.

As she looked out into the storm, the lights in the hall flickered and went out, and she made direct eye contact with the one she knew could have only been Johnathon Storms. She was frozen in place from the soul-piercing gaze of his cold, steel-grey eyes and couldn't believe her ears when she saw him slightly tip his hat and say, "Ma'am," in a gruff voice that boomed like thunder.

"Angela, snap out of it already," said Amanda, startling Angela back into the present moment.

"Amanda!" said Angela, surprised to see Benji and Max back inside, although not so surprised to see them soaking wet. "You almost gave me a heart attack. How did they get back inside?"

"They used the stage entrance."

Angela sat down on the steps leading up to the stage, looking around the room to see that everyone was all right, and kept checking her watch. "What's taking him so long?"

"What's up?" asked Amanda.

"I know he had a big breakfast *and* big lunch at the picnic, but Jacob doesn't usually take *this* long to, you know, finish his business, so to speak."

Amanda stared blankly at Angela for a few short moments, trying to figure out how to word what she wanted to say, knowing that Angela wouldn't take it well either way.

"Jacob's not here."

"Not here? Where is he?"

"Not long before the heavy rainfall, Sabrina thought she heard Kevin rummaging around at the old train station, so she went to greet him, and Jacob went with her. It was like, *right* before the heavy rain started falling, so I'm not surprised you didn't notice."

Angela breathed a sigh of relief. "If Kevin's with them, everything should be fine. If they had any sense, they would've made their way down to the store."

"Then again," said Grandpa, having shown up with Belle, "for as old as that train station is, it's actually rather sturdy."

"Grandpa. Belle," said everyone in their own time.

"Where's Donna?" asked Angela.

Belle reluctantly shook her head and started tearing up and struggled to say anything more than simply, "The river." She sat down beside the stage, hugged her legs close to her face, and cried into her lap.

"What happened?" whispered Angela to Grandpa.

Grandpa started walking towards the far end of the hall and gestured towards Angela to go with her so he could tell as much he knew about what happened as far away from Belle's ears as possible.

"You know what?" said Angela. "Donna's a strong swimmer."

"I agree," said Grandpa. "With any luck—"

"With any luck—"

"No, it's okay, you go."

"I think we're both about to say the same thing anyway."

"Probably. You say it."

"With any luck, she just got swept to the next town over and made it to safety over there."

"Yeah. Here's hoping."

Julie, Max, Benji, and Amanda all talked with each other, hoping that anyone who wasn't there was as safe as possible, and after a long while, Belle felt better and joined the others in their banter.

Wreaking Havoc

The skies grew ever darker as the storm raged on and on and on relentlessly and without repent.

"This looks really bad," said Benji to Julie, looking up at the sky through one of the Town Dinner Hall's many glass walls.

"I can't believe it's become so dark so quick," replied Julie, a quiver in her voice.

"I wonder how long it'll be before the storm passes."

"I wanna go home too," said Julie.

As the two girls sat down, a phenomenal bolt of lightning struck so near that it shook the entire building and almost knocked them off their chairs from the vibration of the blast alone.

"Did that just happen?" asked Julie. "Did we just almost get knocked over by *thunder*?"

"Yeah, I think so," replied Benji, partially stunned.

"I didn't think that *could* happen!"

"The sooner this storm's over, the better," said Benji, readjusting herself.

"I just hope Sabrina and Jacob are okay," said Benji. "Do you think we should maybe go and check on them?"

"No!" said Julie in a rather demanding voice. "We're inside and we're safe. We have to leave others to their own fate.

Whatever this storm has in store for them, they'll have to deal with it themselves."

"I just hope they're safe."

"If they're at the store, they'll be fine, and if they're at the train station, they should be okay too, but if they're anywhere in between—"

"I don't even wanna think about it. Do you think everyone else is all right?"

Benji looked out through the glass panes of the Town Dinner Hall's front doors, noticing that the heavy rain made the buildings in the village look like nothing more than distant blurs, clouded by a wall of thick, grey water.

"In a storm like this," said Julie, "anything could happen."

Sabrina and Jacob were around halfway back from the Inconvenience Store when heavy rain suddenly started to pour.

"What the—?" She stood still, momentarily shocked and amazed by the oncoming storm. When it suddenly hit her just how terrible this could potentially be, she and Jacob both looked at each other and bolted into a full-pelt run, worrying about their parents and the others. However, they'd forced themselves to run so far so fast that by the time they arrived at the abandoned train station, they had worn themselves out, their chests hurting from breathing so deep and so hard.

"I don't think we can make it," she thought aloud as the wind and the rain outside the station became stronger and heavier.

"Let's just wait here for a little bit," she said, going inside the train station, sitting down on one of the benches, pressing her knees up against her chest to try to keep herself warm. "We should've stayed back at the store with Kevin."

Jacob reached into his jacket pocket and pulled out some loose change. "Luckily, I've got some money on me, so we can get something from the vending machine."

Sabrina laughed. "Always thinking ahead, aren't you, Jake?"

"Well, it's not like we've never been in the train station together during a storm before."

"Yeah, but I've got a bad feeling about this one. Like, *really* bad."

The wind and the rain swept heavily over the tin roof of the train station shed, causing all manner of creaks and unpleasant sounds.

"The roof!" exclaimed Sabrina. "It's coming off."

"What?"

"Look," she said, pointing up, having noticed that where they were sitting was getting unusually wet.

The wind was mercilessly bending back the tin sheet that was the roof of the train station, but not loosening its grip or showing any signs of letting go. Branches of trees were banging against the shed, slowly knocking it to pieces, almost as if they were intentionally trying to rip it apart.

"I'm just gonna get some snacks, okay?" said Jacob, scared out of his wits.

"Kevin, come back," called Mr. Jones as Kevin ran out of the Inconvenience Store, worrying about Sabrina's safety. "Ah, kids these days. Do they ever listen?"

"And were you ever so different in your youth?" asked his wife.

"I guess not," replied Mr. Jones, thinking back on his younger days.

"Come on, then; it's best if we lock up. Leave those kids to their own fate."

Mr. and Mrs. Jones locked up the store, making it as secure as they possibly could, taking some supplies out the back, where their sturdy old house was directly attached to the store.

"Should I call that kid's parents, I wonder?"

"Heavens, no! There's enough thunder and lightning out there as it is without you inviting it directly into our home."

The rain poured more heavily, lightning flashed even brighter, and the thunder cracked even louder than it had been doing, so much so that Jacob and Sabrina were having trouble hearing each other, no matter how much they raised their voices over the storm. By now, the tin roof of the train station shed was almost completely torn off, and Jacob and Sabrina were taking cover in the space between one side of the vending machine and the shed wall, as it was the only place not being directly hit by the storm. The calming light-blue light of the vending machine was their only comfort, and even the vending machine was struggling to shine its light in this intense storm.

"Hey," said Sabrina.

"What?"

"I thought I heard something. Wait here."

Sabrina leaned her head out from beside the vending machine, not entirely certain if she'd heard someone call out or not, and just as she leaned over, she saw the glimpse of a boot leaving the shed. "Did I just see that or not?"

"See what?"

"I thought I saw a boot."

"Go check! It's fine, I'll wait here."

"I'll be right back."

Sabrina stood up and made her way to the door, peering out, thinking she could barely make out a large, shadowy figure walking towards the Inconvenience Store.

"*Sabrina!*" Jacob cried out.

As Sabrina turned to see why Jacob called out in such shock, it was as if the whole world started moving in slow motion as she watched the vending machine fall down.

"*Jacob! Move!*" screamed Sabrina, a whirlwind of her worst fears whizzing through her head as she ran to try and stop the vending machine from falling on top of Jacob.

Jacob was frantic and scrambled so much he barely moved at all, trying tirelessly to get away from where the vending machine was falling. However, his efforts were fruitless and in vain as the vending machine came down on top of him. There was nothing he could do, as at that moment—the moment that he, the wall, the floor, and the vending machine all came simultaneously into contact with one another—his life was no more. Sabrina screamed out Jacob's name so loudly that it would have been heard alike by the angels in the high heavens, the dead buried deep below the earth, and every creature in all worlds between.

Merely moments later, Adam came rushing in. "What's going on? What's happened?"

"Help me move the vending machine. It's fallen on Jacob. I think he's ..."

"Oh, no. No, no, no, no, no."

Adam and Sabrina did their best to lift the vending machine off Jacob but did little more than manage to half roll it over. Adam kept aggressively shoving it, shouldering it, and doing all he could to move it off Jacob, who was bleeding profusely, his torso crushed and his arms and legs severely broken.

"Jacob," called Sabrina lightly as she knelt down beside him.

"Oh, Sabrina, no," said Adam, placing his hands on Sabrina's shoulders.

"Jacob, wake up," she said, lightly shaking Jacob's body.

"Sabrina, no. He's gone. I'm sorry. He's gone," said Adam as he noticed Jacob's lifeless corpse starting to shake uncontrollably.

"What's happening to him?"

"All the nerves in his body are firing off uncontrollably. Ancient healers used to think it was the soul leaving the body."

"Okay." Sabrina nodded as she tried to accept Jacob's fate, a river of tears uncontrollably streaming down her face. "What do we do now?"

"We take Jacob's body back to the village and face the music."

Leaving Unprepared

Sabrina and Adam had just arrived at the Town Dinner Hall, Adam carrying Jacob's corpse. Sabrina suggested using the stage entrance, as it was better protected from the elements.

"You're right. With winds like this, there's no telling how hard it'll be to shut those doors once they're open."

Once inside, Adam laid Jacob's lifeless body down on of the tables.

Angela, in a panicked and anguished wreck, tried resuscitating him.

"Angela," said Grandpa, in a soft and reassuring voice. "Angela dear, it's too late; he's gone," he said, holding back tears. "Julie, could you get the blankets? They're up in the loft."

Julie quietly got up and went to retrieve the blankets.

"Jacob, wake up," cried Angela, shaking Jacob's corpse by its shoulders. "Please, Jacob. It's your mum; it's Angela."

"It was the vending machine," added Adam. "It happened right before I got there. Sabrina and I did all that we could to get it off him."

"*You!*" scowled Angela, her gaze now fixed on Adam, an accusatory finger pointed directly at him. "*You* did this to my boy."

"No. Angela, it wasn't like that at all," said Sabrina, her words unheard.

"Everything was *fine* before *you* came here, and then *you* happened. *You* came here, and you brought the *storms* with you. For as long as I've lived in this village, we've never—*never*—had weather *this bad* before, and then *you* show up, bringing this bad weather in your wake, killing my boy. How *dare* you. Now go *back* to your house, pack up your belongings, and *get out!* I don't ever want to see you here again."

Reluctant to argue, Adam made his way out of the Town Dinner Hall, unknowingly accompanied by Amanda, who sneaked out almost immediately after him when no one was looking.

Back at the house where he'd been staying, Adam showered, put on some clean clothes, and started packing his bags. He looked at clothes and what he needed to pack, thinking of all the memories he'd built since he'd been here, each item holding some special significance, reminding him of something from the past year. He heard a noise.

"Is someone there?" he asked as he poked his head out of his room and looked down into the living room.

"It's just me," came Amanda's voice from the kitchen.

"Oh, Amanda. It's you. What are you doing here?" he said as he walked to the kitchen to meet her.

"I've always known Angela to be a little emotionally unstable, particularly in regard to Jacob, but I've never seen her go off like that at *anyone* before. Just wondering if you were okay?"

"It's fine. I'm the new guy, and she needed a scapegoat. No one here knows me as well as anyone knows everyone else here. I can only imagine the thought processes she's going through right now," said Adam as he forced back tears.

"Are you really going to leave?"

"Trust me. I've had more than enough misadventures in my life to know when to leave, and this is definitely one of those times."

"If you wait a couple of days, she might come around."

"I don't wanna push my luck. I've pushed it before and learnt my lesson the hard way. I feel like after her emotional outburst, my being here'll just make things all that much more awkward."

"But what if you *not* being here made things even *more* awkward?"

Adam paused for a moment, taking in what Amanda had just said, weighing up the odds of staying versus leaving and decided that it would indeed be best to leave.

"It's just that there's somethings that I have to do. Things that only I can do."

"Things that you can't do here?" asked Amanda softly.

"Exactly," said Adam.

"You'll be missed, that's for sure."

Getting a little choked up and teary-eyed, Adam couldn't bring himself to say much more than "Yep."

"Um ... you want me to put the kettle on? I could make you some tea."

"Yes, that sounds great. Let's have some tea. I'll keep packing, and you call me when the tea's ready."

"That's generally how it works." Amanda smiled softly as she turned on the kettle, and Adam went to pack more of his things.

After a few minutes, Amanda called out to Adam that the tea was ready, but there came no reply. "Adam?" she called out. "Adam!"

She went to his room, but his things were gone, his bed made, his room as undisturbed now as it was when he first arrived, as if he'd never been there at all. A conflict of emotions tangled within her, between being angry that he left without a word and relieved that he'd successfully gone. All she could say was "Huh. So that's how it is."

Solitude

S obbing uncontrollably, a river of tears streaming down her face, Sabrina walked hastily along the still-wet path towards what Jacob always referred to as the Inconvenience Store. She walked so fast, she occasionally caught herself speeding up to a light run.

"Bet you can't catch me," echoed the memory of Jacob's voice in her mind, but no matter how hard she tried, she couldn't outrun his memory.

"Go away," she cried as she started to run. "Just leave me alone."

She bolted into a full-pelt run, faster than she'd ever run before, running so far so fast that by the time her tears had stopped and she'd calmed down a little, she wasn't too sure where she was, disoriented from running while crying. She looked around for a bit and after a while saw an enormous lone tree in the middle of a field atop a slight hill.

"Oh, this place."

It was a place she remembered from her childhood where her parents took her for picnics on nice days when they still lived at the next town over.

Sabrina walked over to the tree and sat under its shade, her back to the trunk, surprised that the ground was as dry as it was, supposing that side of the tree must have received a good amount of sunlight over the past few days. She looked off to her right and saw the next town over, wondering what the experiences of the people there were like during the storm. Did they have their own Adam? Their own Jacob? Their own Belle and Donna? She wondered what Kevin was doing and if he'd heard about Donna.

The train whistled as she sat there, and she looked off to the left to see a steam train billowing smoke as she wondered what they'd do about the landslide. She squinted and saw that it wasn't a passenger train but was pulling some specialised equipment which could've only possibly been for dealing with the landslide. "Oh, I guess *that's* what they're doing about the landslide."

She wondered about Adam too. Did he take the train? Did he leave into the city via ferry, as Jacob and Angela so often did? Did he leave the same way as Joshua and go "far beyond where the horizon lies," whatever that meant?

Sabrina hugged her legs closer to herself so she could rest her head on her knees, closing her eyes, wanting to cry but knowing she couldn't when she was very surprised to hear an all-too-familiar voice. "Hello, Sabrina."

"Jacob?" she said, opening her eyes to an unusually bright light.

It was undeniably Jacob, surrounded by a strong light and dark-blue glowing aura.

"You're glowing," she said as she stood up.

"I'm in a better place now."

Sabrina wasn't sure how to react to that statement, so she just nodded her head and smiled. "Okay. What's it like ... over there?"

"It's everything you could possibly imagine, Sabrina, and so much more."

"Since when do *you* talk like *that*?" Sabrina laughed.

"Yeah, okay. I thought that's just how maybe people talked when they got here, but I guess not, huh? Honestly, it's *awesome* over this side. Remember that roundabout thing we used to play on in that park, where you spin around then see who can hold on the longest?"

"Yeah? What about it? Didn't they move it or something?"

"Yeah, I think they took it out and put a house there or something because too many kids were getting injured falling off it."

"What about it?"

"It's here! You can spin around on that thing all day long if you like and fall off as many times as you like, and it *never hurts*, and you never *get* hurt, because that's just what it's like here. Honestly, it's awesome!"

Sabrina couldn't help but laugh. "I miss your enthusiasm."

"You miss my enthusiasm?"

"Yeah."

"I might not be there anymore, Sabrina, but my enthusiasm will always be there. It'll live on through you, if you allow it."

"Okay," said Sabrina with a forced nod and an awkward smile.

"Anyway, you should probably get going. We've been here longer you realise, and your mum's probably getting worried. Kevin's fine. Joshua says hi, and we're still looking for Donna. It's like she's missing in action both over here *and* over there. It's quite the conundrum."

"Joshua? You mean, he's—"

"No. It's not like that. He just prays *a lot* and is forever sending his love to the village."

"But how—"

"Things work differently on this side. Everything's so much clearer, it's insane. I've tried appearing to Mum, but she's just not ready yet, I guess."

Sabrina nodded again, this time more easily. "I'll tell her you said hi."

Jacob laughed and said it was best to wait until she'd calmed down and that he wanted to greet her in his own time.

"That's okay. I understand."

"Anyway, Sabrina, I can only do this so often and only for so long each time. I'm surprised it's lasted this long, to be honest, but there's not really any distractions up here, and other than Mum, I'm closer to you than anyone else in the village, so that probably explains it. Other than that, I really do think you should get going. Seems like your mum's preparing to cook one of her famous roast lamb dinners. If you leave now, you should get home just in time for it be served."

"You're right," she said, looking towards the next town over. "I guess I'll go that way. It seems like the most direct route."

"Sure. Say hi to Kevin for me."

"I will."

"I'll see you again, Sabrina."

"I'll see you again too."

Sabrina wiped a tear from her eye and headed off home via the next town over, her spirits now much higher than they were before. "Thanks for everything, Jake."

Fallen from Grace

It was an unusually cold day for this time of year as the remains of the storm's grey clouds lingered menacingly over the village, hanging low and sporadically stretched from horizon to horizon. The village was unrecognisably destroyed; only the Town Dinner Hall, Grandma and Grandpa's place, Adam's old house, and the cinema remained. Even the song of the woodlands had changed, the wind travelling through heavily changed, now-unfamiliar terrain.

Angela knocked on Grandpa's front door, a picnic basket hanging on one arm and a broad, artificial smile forced across her face.

"Oh, it's you," said Grandpa. "Come in, dear. We've got a lot to talk about."

"Grandpa, I'm so glad to see you," said Angela, as she walked hurriedly to the kitchen where she knew Grandma would be. "Oh, Grandma, nice to see you too. The weather we've been having's been so strange lately, hasn't it?"

Angela sat at the kitchen table, her forced smile unwavering, put down the picnic basket, opened it, and took out some freshly—although poorly—baked scones.

"Don't they smell great?" she said as she placed them on a plate. And smell great they did, although they didn't look nearly as appetizing as they smelled.

"They look, uh ..." began Grandma, concerned.

"They smell great," interrupted Grandpa as he placed one on his plate, ready to slice it open and some jam and cream to either side.

Angela put her hand on Grandma's shoulder, distracting her from saying anything else. "Grandma, looks can be deceiving. You of all people should know that."

"So, Angela," started Grandma, "is ... is there anything you wanna talk about?"

Angela looked around as if scanning the inside of her mind for anything else that she wanted to talk about and seemed to draw a blank. "Nope. Nothing that I can think of. Why? Is there something that you want to hear me say?"

She laughed, trying to keep the situation calm. Grandma and Grandpa politely, although awkwardly, laughed along with her.

"I've made enough for the whole village," she said, pointing to her picnic basket.

"Great," said Grandma and Grandpa supportively, looking at each other and then at the basket.

"No, really, I have," she said, opening the basket, revealing enough scones for more than ten villages worth of people. "I baked them last night in the Town Dinner Hall. My Jacob's going to *love* these when he gets back home from the store."

The room became unusually silent as Grandma and Grandpa looked at each other in shock for what seemed like a small eternity, although in reality was perhaps only a matter of a few seconds.

"Just *love* them," continued Angela. "Anyway, best be going. I've got scones to deliver."

"Uh. Right you are," said Grandpa as he stood up and saw Angela to the door.

"All right, see you later, Dad. Hope the weather improves."

"Me too, dear. Me too."

Where We Once Sat

Belle stood by that one particular park bench beside the river, the clouds still hanging unusually low in the sky, staring blankly into the river's still, calm waters. She wondered what had become of Donna, the events of that night replaying over and over in her mind, forever thinking what she could've done differently but didn't. She looked down the river towards the next town over, wondering if Donna may have made it down there. As for herself, she thought she might go and see Kevin later, to see how badly the other village had been damaged, and, as vain as she knew her hope was, find out something—anything—about Donna. She even imagined, although she knew falsely, that she and Donna might be reunited.

"Hello," said Benji, her usual friendly self.

Belle jumped slightly before realising it was Benji.

"Ah, sorry. I guess I really do somehow sneak up people unwittingly."

Belle smiled. "You really do."

"So, I guess this is where it happened, huh?"

"Yeah," said Belle with a slow nod. "This is where I lost Donna."

"Oh," said Benji, surprised. "Sorry, I didn't mean ... I mean, I just meant that ... I mean. Eh, it doesn't matter."

Realising her error, Belle insisted Benji continue what she meant.

"Well, before I continue, I'm sorry for your loss, and I hope she's okay wherever she's ended up."

Belle nodded. "It's okay. Go on."

"I just meant that this is where most of us were when that storm began. Jacob and Sabrina had just gone to the old train station, and then the rain started. That's when everything started to change."

Belle still nodded intermittently, acknowledging Benji's words, but kept staring blankly into the river, her mind a jumble of thoughts, recounting that day's events.

"Belle?"

"Huh? Oh, sorry. Just thinking."

"About what?"

"About how if we'd listened to Grandpa, if we'd been more decisive, if we'd just made our minds up quicker one way or the other, Donna might still be here."

"Belle," said Benji solemnly, "if you'd gone down past the tracks like Grandpa said, the landslide would've likely gotten the better of both of you. As I understand, it went all the way from here down to the station. Not to mention they'll be cleaning up that mess for a while. You're lucky to still be here and lucky that there's at least *hope* for Donna's survival."

"We used to sit together at lunchtime almost every day on the steps of Grandma and Grandpa's front porch."

"I know. I think everyone knows that." said Benji. "I've never had a friendship with anyone in the village like Sabrina had with Jacob or like you have with Donna, but if it's okay with you—and I don't at all mean to offer myself as a replacement—today I could sit with you on the steps, if you like."

"I appreciate the offer, but ..."

"What is it?"

"Just ... not today."

"Oh? May I ask why? If that's not too intrusive of a question, that is."

"Huh? Oh no, not at all. The steps always seemed so close, I'd often surprise myself with how quickly I got there, but I went to sit on them this morning, and I don't think those steps have ever looked further away to me in my life. They're only just down the road from where I live, but I just couldn't bring myself to go and sit on those steps today. It even almost felt as if a higher power was preventing me from doing it, so I came here instead. But you're more than welcome to sit with me there on other days. Once I'm comfortable with it again."

"As for right now, how about Kevin?"

"I was thinking about going to see him a little later," replied Belle.

"Well, then let's go see him now, and by the time we get there, it'll be a little later."

"Yeah, right," said Belle.

Benji put her arm around Belle's neck, and Belle put her arm around Benji's waist, and they both made their way on to the next town over, both starting to be a little happier than they were before.

Above them, the clouds started to part, and blue skies appeared.

It Still Hurts

Sabrina had just walked away from the tree, reinvigorated by her experience with Jacob's apparition, and was headed back to the village by way of the next town over. She thought she'd stop in and see Kevin on the way home. About halfway down the hill, Sabrina stopped to take in what the village looked from that high above, noticing that the layout wasn't entirely different from her own village, noting the colours were more muted and generally quite neutral. As she got closer and closer, for all the similarities she could see between the two places, she also began to realise neither place was at all like the other.

"Sabrina?" called one of the grown-ups. "You're from the village just over that way, right?"

"Yeah. I was just on that hill up there. Thought I'd make my way back through here, rather than go around the way I came. See what Kevin's up to, if he's here."

"Oh, I remember when you'd go and have picnics up there with your parents. How are they?"

"My parents? They're fine. I mean, we're all staying at the Town Dinner Hall after that hideously bad weather recently, but we're okay?"

"And Jacob? How's Jacob?"

Sabrina froze hearing Jacob's name, unsure of how to react, looking back at the tree, thinking maybe the experience she just had wasn't as healing as she thought it was.

"Is everything okay?"

Sabrina fought with thoughts in her head, one telling her to say that Jacob was fine—after all, based on what just happened, he was—which might lead to awkward social exchanges in the future, which Sabrina would prefer to avoid at all costs, or confront her emotions head-on and tell this lady—someone Sabrina had vague memories of from her childhood—the complete truth.

As tears streamed down her cheeks, with a quiver in her voice and trying her best to keep herself together, Sabrina said, "Jacob's dead. He was crushed under the vending machine during the storm."

The woman's face turned from delight to shear dread and she covered her gaping mouth with her hand. "Oh my gosh, Sabrina. I'm so sorry. I had no idea. I ... I don't know what to say."

"No, it's okay. It wasn't your fault. You didn't know."

"You know what?" said the lady awkwardly. "How about you run along, no? You know where Kevin's house is. Same place as it always was. Um. Actually, I'm not sure if he's in today, but if he's not, he's just gone into the city, and I know you know your way there, so ... um ... yeah. You have a good, um, you have a good day, Sabrina. I'll be seeing you next time."

"Good day, ma'am," said Sabrina, and she went on her way.

Sabrina knocked on Kevin's door and called out his name a few times, although no answer came. She just stood there, staring blankly at the door and at her shoes, wondering whether she should venture off into the city by herself or just go back to the village. She raised her hand to the door one last time, although she didn't really know why, and knocked lightly without much effort, half-heartedly calling out Kevin's name again before deciding to just head back to the village.

Benji and Belle were walking along towards the next town over, Belle feeling much better, when Benji noticed something. "Hey, is that Sabrina?"

"Yeah, I think it is."

"Hey!"

They both smiled and waved energetically, happy to see their friend. Sabrina half-heartedly smiled and waved back. Benji noted that she must still be upset over what happened to Jacob.

"And to have witnessed with her own eyes, firsthand, too," added Belle, thinking about Donna as she glanced back at the river.

Sabrina approached them and told Belle that she was sure it'd only be a matter of time before Donna was found.

"I hope so."

"Kevin's not home, by the way, if that's where you're going. Some lady told me he's likely gone into the city."

"Oh," said Belle. "Then let's go into the city."

"Yeah," agreed Benji.

"Are you coming?" asked Belle.

"No, thank you. I think I might just go for a walk. I might go up to the other train station and see how well it weathered the storm."

"Ah," began Belle. "The weather's improving, so I think it'll be a nice walk."

"Yeah, me too. See you this afternoon, I guess."

Benji and Belle looked at each other, both with a mischievous look in their eye. "Perhaps more like this evening," said Benji.

"Uh, yeah, well, anyway, I'm sure none of your parents would want you to be home too late, I guess."

Benji and Belle both laughed.

"Of course not," said Belle.

"All right, we'll see you this evening," reaffirmed Benji.

"Wait," said Belle. "We'll see you," she began, thinking about how to word what she wanted to say. "I've got it. We'll see you when we see you."

Sabrina smiled, waved briefly, and went on her way.

Sibling Rivalry

Julie and Max were sitting on the front steps of the Town Dinner Hall, wondering what the future would bring and how long it would be before the village would be back to normal again, if ever.

"It's not the same without Adam here anymore," said Julie.

"Yeah. Do you think he knew we were twins?"

"Probably not," laughed Julie. "I think most people assume we're not. I mean, you're noticeably taller, and for some reason, I look marginally older."

"Yeah, I always thought that was weird. People do think you're the older sibling."

"Not that there's many new people here that often."

"I mean, when was the last time someone new came here before Adam?"

"Yeah, I wonder." Julie smiled, actually thinking about it, struggling to remember. "Wait, when *was* the last someone new came to the village?"

They looked at each other, their eyes wide and eyebrows raised with concern, confusion, and curiosity.

"Grandpa would know," said Max as he stood up. "Are you coming?"

"Sure."

Grandpa had seen Julie and Max walking towards his house through the living room window and was already at the door when they arrived. "What's up, kids? How can I help you?"

"We were just wondering," began Julie, "if you remember who the last person was to visit the village," continued Max, "before Adam," they finished in unison.

Grandpa smirked, raised an eyebrow, and took a sip from his cup of coffee. "So, you don't remember, huh?"

"Well, no," they said. "That's why we're here."

"Why don't you take a trip over to the cinema, go through the files in the offices, and see what you can find over there?"

Confused, they both looked at each other.

"I'm serious. Go check," he said with a smile and a light laugh.

Julie turned to Max. "I'll see you there."

"See me there? I mean, we're going together, right?"

Before Max knew it, Julie had bolted off towards the old cinema, kicking up plenty of dust.

"Hey! No fair," said Max as he raced off after her.

Grandpa laughed as he watched the two of them race of towards the cinema. "I hope they like what they find."

Above the village, the clouds were parting, blue sky and sunshine slowing being revealed.

Now at the cinema, and out of breath, Julie and Max took a moment to catch their breath, both noting that the weather was slowly improving.

"I really hope that the worst of the bad weather is behind us now," said Max, his eyes bound skyward.

"Me too. I mean, I think we *all* saw Johnathan. It was the most chilling feeling I've ever experienced in my life."

"Yeah, I know exactly what you mean. And to think what happened to Jacob and Donna."

"Do you think we'll ever see Donna again?"

"Honestly? My gut feeling says no."

"Mine too, I'm sorry to say," said Julie with a heavy heart. "However, I've got this feeling that—"

"We'll definitely see Adam again," they both finished in unison.

"Shall we go in?" asked Julie as she walked in through the automatic doors.

"That's strange," said Max. "I don't remember this place having automatic doors. I thought it had those old-fashioned revolving doors."

"Old fashioned?" asked Julie with a raised eyebrow. "You mean like those doors over there and there?" She pointed to the revolving doors either side of the automatic doors.

"Yeah, but I thought—" he said, stopping mid-sentence, baffled.

"Well, clearly you thought wrong. I've never really paid much attention to such things myself."

"And since when has there been a vending machine in here?" he said quite loudly, storming over to the brand-new vending machine. "Oh," he said, looking it over, "this is similar to the ones up at the regular train station. What's it doing *here*?"

"Somebody probably just put it there."

"Yeah, but who?"

Julie and Max looked at each other, both realising that neither of them knew anything about the vending machines.

"I have no memory of there *not* being a vending machine at the old train station, and yet I know nothing about it. Not even a memory of other people talking about it," said Jacob.

"I don't know why, but I always just assumed it was Grandpa that tended to it."

"Speaking of Grandpa, let's go up to the office by the projection room and see what he was talking about."

For an office that wasn't frequented that much, it was surprisingly clean and not nearly as dusty as both Julie and Max had imagined it was going to be. The walls were white. In the corner sat a typical office desk with two drawers under it, a filing cabinet to the right of it, and a few wall shelves here and there. On the back of the office's door was an open-top pouch, full of various types of articles and writings and so on, although nothing of particular interest. Julie noticed a set of keys laid upon the desk, and she immediately used them in the office desk's top drawer, where they fit perfectly. The drawer was full of some envelopes, one in particular bulging more than most. It was a mustard-yellow colour and had an elastic band around either side of it. Julie took it out of the drawer, removed the bands, and opened it. It was chock-a-block full of old photos of the village and various people who had come and gone.

"Hey, Max, look."

"What is it? Oh, cool. Hey, show me some."

Julie handed about half of them to Max, and he pulled up a folding chair that was leaning against a wall and sat beside her.

"Hey, is that Grandpa?" asked Max as he pointed to one of the old photos.

"Oh my gosh. It *does* look like Grandpa."

"And I think that's Angela."

"She's so young!"

"I know, right?"

"And here's one of her pregnant with Jacob."

"Wait, how do you know it's Jacob?"

"She only has one kid. Who else would it be, dummy?"

"Oh, yeah. Right. Heh."

Going through the old photos, they realised that the village had quite a rich and varied history. Much richer than what they had imagined in their relatively short lives.

"There's so many people here I don't recognise," said Julie.

"I know, right? I was just thinking the same thing."

After each of them had gone through a few more photos, making idle comments on most of them, Max suggested that they sort them out and put them order, as they didn't seem to be in any particular order.

"What do you think I've been doing this whole time?" she said as she gestured towards a pile every bit as messy as Max's.

"Um, I dunno. Maybe, *not* sorting them out and putting them in order?"

"Yeah, okay. You got me."

Between them, they then decided how to sort the photos into different piles, putting a separate pile for each person they definitely knew, another pile for people they *thought* they knew, and a third and final pile for people they definitely didn't know, the first pile eventually being grouped on a person-by-person basis.

"Hey, look on the back," said Max. "Some of these are named and dated. See? Cecilia and Adam, twenty-four years."

"Let me see." Angela flipped the photo back and forth once or twice and said, "I think that's how old they in the picture, not the date."

"Wait. That's Grandma and Grandpa."

"Grandpa's name is Adam? Huh. And I thought Grandma's name was Cecil."

"I guess it's short for Cecelia."

"I guess so."

The two of them kept sorting the photos for more hours than they realised had passed.

Earth Song

The weather was gradually improving, and Sabrina had decided to take a stroll to the other train station to see how bad the damage there was and make inquiries about changed train timetables and so on.

"Oh, Sabrina," called Grandpa as he saw Sabrina passing by, "what's going on? You headed somewhere?"

"Yeah, ah, just, um, the other train station," she said, her hand, still in her hoodie pocket, pointed in the direction she was aiming.

"You know, I think that place probably weathered the storm pretty well."

"Yeah, probably, but I'd still like to go and check for myself, you know?"

"No, I get it. There's nothing quite like firsthand experience to teach you about the world, right?"

"Right," she replied after a short pause before heading onwards.

"Oh, uh, and if you see Angela—" he began.

"No, it's okay, Grandpa. I know what Angela's like. Other than Jacob, I think I probably know her better than anyone."

"Speaking of Jacob," said Grandpa awkwardly, "how you holding up?"

Sabrina smiled at awkward attempts at caring. "It's okay, Grandpa," she said, thinking back on her experiences by the tree on the hill earlier that day. "He's in a better place now. Like, *so* much better."

"I'm sure he is," said Grandpa, relieved.

"Oh, and—" began Sabrina, unsure if she should continue, "Joshua says hi," she finished with a mischievous grin and a slight bob of her head before walking off. "Okay, bye, Grandpa. See you this afternoon."

"Huh," began Grandpa, slightly confused. "Joshua," he finished with a contented smile, "I'm glad to hear he's doing well."

About halfway to the other train station, Sabrina came upon something seemingly out of place on the side of the road: a large blue box. Wondering if it was what she thought it was, she increased her pace, although she made sure to approach with caution.

"It is. I don't believe it," she said, now approaching more hastily. "It's a vending machine."

She looked around, curious that it was in such a remote location and even called out "hello" a few times to see if anyone was around.

As strange as it was that a vending machine stood in the middle of nowhere, Sabrina couldn't quite shake that awkward sense of familiarity exuding from it. She looked back down towards the village, thinking of the old train station. Her face scrunched up; one eyebrow raised.

"It can't be? Can it?"

Perplexed, she pushed one of its buttons, which lit up and caused a small digital screen above the money slot to read: "Please insert coins."

Ever more confused, but still entirely curious, Sabrina pulled out some loose change from her pockets and purchased a drink.

"Thank you. Please come again," read the orange text of the digital display.

Sabrina continued on her way and occasionally looked back over her shoulder to see that the vending machine was still there as she walked off.

A little while later, Sabrina had made it to her destination, noting that there was very little damage to the station, both inside and out.

"Sorry, dear. No trains today," came a little old lady's voice from behind the counter. "Well, not for a while, actually. Because of the landslide, you know?"

"Huh? Oh yeah, I know. It's okay. I'm from the village just down the road from here and thought I'd come and see what the damage was like."

"Oh, you're from *that* village. Heard you didn't fare too well down there."

"Yeah. Thankfully the town's main building, the Town Dinner Hall, is still standing, so most of us will be biding our time there until repairs are made."

"I've got good news for ya, kid."

"Oh?"

"Help is on its way."

"It is?"

"When a train came by earlier today to assess the damage after hearing about the landslide, they had other damage assessors on board to survey the perimeter, and a few of them noted the severe damage at your particular village and sent word out for help."

"But how ... But the landslide, so how ...?"

"Oh. One train from either direction met halfway after clearing the landslide, and because it's two trains on one track, they thought it best they *both* went back, left the tracks open for a day or two while they sort out the schedule of what needs to be done and how to go about doing it. Then once they'd returned, they relayed messages via telegram to people who might be able to help, then word got back that some construction workers from the city will come over and help as soon as they can. Likely no earlier than lunchtime tomorrow."

"Oh, thanks for the info. I'll tell Grandpa."

"Grandpa? He still lives down there?" asked the lady, pointing in the direction of the village.

"Yeah? So, you know Grandpa?" asked Sabrina, a little concerned.

"Yeah, I know Grandpa."

The old lady looked around as if trying to find certain information inside her own head, started counting on her fingers, and then asked Sabrina how old she was.

"Nearly fifteen."

"Huh," said the old lady, as if a little confused. "Sometimes I can't help but wonder where the time goes." She sighed.

"O ... kayyyy ..."

"Sorry, kid, I didn't mean to upset you or nothin' like that. It's just that I've been here so long, the days, weeks, months, and years all sort of just end up blurring into each other, you know?"

"Not really."

"Too young, I guess. Anyway, a lot of the trees that fell in that landslide'll be turned into lumber, and a lot of that lumber'll be used to repair the houses in your village."

"I guess that's just the circle of life, huh?"

"Sure is, kid."

"But I feel kind of bad for all the animals who lost their homes in that storm."

"Wouldn't worry about it, kid. There ain't nothin' you can do about that. I mean, it's sweet that you care, but at the end of the day, *you* gotta take care of *you* and never mind so much about how other people go about their business. What happens, happens. Simply, it is the way of things."

Sabrina nodded, acknowledging what the old lady said, right before she noticed a vending machine in the station identical to the one she passed on the way to the station.

"Has that always been here?" asked Sabrina.

"That one has, but the one you see the markings of on the floor next to it? It isn't always there. I rent them, so it depends on what I can afford from one month to the next. I sent the other one off when the trains came earlier because with the reduced patronage I'll be seeing for the next few days, if not a month or more, there's no way I'd be able to afford both of them. Why? You want something?"

"No, it's okay. I got something on the way here," she said, showing the drink she purchased from the vending machine on her way there. "I guess I'll be off now."

"See you next time, kiddo."

"It's Sabrina."

"Okay. See you next time, Sabrina."

"Bye."

Sabrina was almost back at the village and paused, as she didn't remember passing any vending machine on the way back. She turned to look but was already far enough down the hill that she couldn't see much past the top of it. She pulled out the drink she picked up from it earlier, quietly pondering its existence before putting back into her pocket and then casually wandering to the Town Dinner Hall, where she told everybody of the good news she received at the train station.

Gone

Not quite a week had passed. The weather was clearing up, slowly getting better and better day by day, and Angela was wide awake and ready to face the day.

"Jacob!" she called out. After no answer, she called out again, got a little frustrated, and went to Jacob's room. "Oh, that boy, sleeping in again."

Angela was a little surprised to see an empty bed, but in a small way relieved when she the sounds of children playing in the street drifted through the bedroom window. "Oh, I guess he got up early and went to play with his friends."

She finished getting ready, left the house, and decided to see if she could quickly find Jacob, to see if he wanted to join her for a day trip into the city.

After looking here and there in a few spots where she thought he might be, she decided it'd be best to leave him wherever he was and went to ask Amanda if she'd like to join her in the city for the day.

"Hi, Amanda," said Angela as Amanda answered the door.

"Oh, Angela. Hi. Is everything okay?"

"Yeah, I'm great," she said with a beaming, yet clearly painfully forced smile. "I thought you might like to join me while I go for a day trip into the city. I can't find Jacob *any*where. I guess he's out playing with Sabrina or some of the other kids somewhere. Although it is a little unusual for him to be up this early, but not entirely unheard of now that I think about it."

Amanda hesitantly agreed to go, excusing herself to first go and get her things before she joined Angela, all the while wondering what to say about Jacob or if she should say anything at all.

As they headed of, they saw Grandpa out for his morning walk. "Oh, hey girls, how's it going? You two off into the city today?"

"Oh, you know," began Angela, "I went to arouse Jacob, but I guess he got up early and went to play with his friends. I mean, I know Jacob isn't actually that fond of the city except for when I let him take the shopping cart, but I really just enjoy the company, and I didn't want to disturb Jacob if he's off somewhere collecting leaves or something, so I asked Amanda here instead."

"Okay. You two girls enjoy your day."

The two of them continued onward, and Angela asked Amanda about Adam.

"Well, actually," she said awkwardly after a short pause, not quite knowing how to answer. "Ah, actually, you know what? I haven't seen Adam in a few days."

"Oh, really?" Angela smiled. "I think it's healthy for couples to spend some time apart. It'll make you both appreciate each other that much more."

Trying not to think back on how Adam left so suddenly the other night, Amanda was struggling to hold back tears.

"You know, Angela—" began Amanda, the subtle hint of a combination of anger and despair in her voice as she remembered the words spoken to Adam on the fateful night, but also trying to acknowledge the fact that Angela genuinely didn't seem to remember the events of that night. "Sometimes people just leave. They just pack up their stuff and they go, without saying a word."

"Oh, honey, it's fine," said Angela with a dismissive wave of her hand. "People like Adam don't leave for long. The way he looks at you? Believe me, that boy's definitely coming back."

"You really think so, huh? Has anyone *ever* come back to the village after a storm like that?"

Angela took Amanda's hand, tilted her head, and smiled lovingly. "Historically, no. But Adam's different, you'll see. I've had a good feeling about him since the day he first arrived here."

Now at the old train station, Amanda mentioned that she'd like to stop in and get something from the vending machine for a snack or two later in the day.

Inside, both of them were surprised to see the absence of a vending machine, save for the markings on the floor where the machine once stood.

"What's that?" asked Angela as she noticed a small brown item on the floor. Angela approached the item with cautious curiosity. "Jacob's wallet?" she said softly, a weak stutter in her voice.

"Oh, I'm sure whoever's wallet it is, they'll come back for it when they realise they've lost it."

Angela knelt in front of the wallet in total silence, her gaze fixed upon it.

"Is everything okay?" asked Angela slowly, as she sat on the bench next to the machine.

An influx of memories thunderously bombarded Angela's mind as one tear after another started streaming down her face into a river of tears. "Jacob. Adam. Oh, Amanda, I ..."

"It's okay. It's okay."

Amanda sat on the bench and put her arm around Angela, who was blubbering uncontrollably, almost entirely lost for words.

"What am I supposed to do without my baby boy?"

"We'll just have to keep on living our lives. Our ordinary, everyday lives like we always have."

Angela sat up straight, nodded her head, and wiped away her tears. After regaining her composure, she asked, "So, now what?"

"Well, we *were* going into the city, so I mean, if you still want to go?"

"Actually, you know what? I think I'd like that. I *need* that. Would you still like to come with me?"

"Oh my gosh, of course. If you'll still have me."

"Absolutely. I could do with the company. I can tell you all about Jacob over lunch. I feel like I've got a lot I need to let out, if you don't mind me leaning on you, that is."

"Not at all," said Amanda. "I'd love to be your leaning post."

"Okay then."

"Okay."

The two of them left the old train station, headed off into the city, and did their best to enjoy the rest of their day.

In a Large, Loud City (Where Something Almost Always Happens)

Belle and Benji were walking down the dark forest path, away from the river, the store, the old train station, and the village, towards the ferry that crossed the other river that separated their village from the city.

"Don't you just love this part of the walk?" asked Belle.

"Other than the darkly coloured plant life that varies wildly from around the rest of the village's area, I don't particularly see anything special about it.

"What? You don't see open book pages at the end of the forest path?" She smiled, mildly shocked. "Here, look I'll show you. It's the perfect time of day for it too."

Belle pointed out that from where they stood, if you looked closely at the trees at the opening of the end of the forest path, it looked like a large open book.

"And when the leaves blow past or birds fly across the opening at *just* the right time, in *just* the right way, it looks as if a page of the book is turning."

As Belle spoke, almost as if in answer to her words, a light breeze blew some leaves from one side of the forest path to the other as some birds flew across at the same time as well.

"Oh!" said Benji, excited. "I see it. Wow."

"Isn't in wonderful?" asked Belle. "It's almost as if it's indicating that a new chapter of our lives has begun. Not to mention that when I pass through there, it feels like I'm walking through the pages from one book to another, and I find that feeling completely invigorating. But it is a relief when I come back to the village. The feeling here is cosier somehow."

Benji smiled. "I had no idea you felt that way. And as for a new chapter of our lives started, given everything that's happened lately, I almost feel like a new *volume* of our lives is starting."

"Yeah," replied Belle, becoming ever so slightly more sombre. "I wonder what Adam and Donna are doing now. Or if Donna's even still alive?"

"Don't give up hope, Belle. There's no sign whatsoever that she's dead, so there's no reason to think she's anything other than alive."

"I know."

They continued onward, approaching the edge of the Dividing River—named because of its dividing the land between the villages' area and the cities' area—just as the ferry pulled up to the riverbank.

Belle and Benji both excitedly waved at the ferryman as the ferry pulled up, and he smiled and waved back.

"Oh, it's the younger one," said Benji with a smile "He's so nice."

"I know, right? The whole family's nice, actually."

"Yeah, but this one is *particularly* nice."

Before Belle had a chance to react, the particularly nice ferryman asked, "Off to the city today, ladies?"

"Yes," they replied, handing over a few shillings' payment each as they stepped on board.

The two girls hurried toward the front of the ferry to enjoy the wind in their hair as they crossed the river.

At the other side of the river, Belle and Benji happily alighted the ferry, excited to spend a good deal of their day in the city and wondering if they would perhaps chance upon Kevin while they were there.

As they walked into the main street, they were struck by the ominous and eerie mist that filled the air, the mysterious silhouettes that populated the streets, almost as if they were ghosts of folk from days gone by.

"I guess it's always a little strange when you're in a place where no one knows your name," said Benji.

"Yeah. Where do you supposed we'd find Kevin if he were about?"

"He likes drinking, right? So probably in one of those waterhole-type places."

"Oh, right. The Fuzzy Duck, or something?"

"I thought it was The Three Flapping Ducks?"

"Yeah, that's it! I remember as you open the door, it knocks a bell that pulls on a string that makes the wooden ducks outside the door flap their wings."

"If we get inside, we can get away from this incessant fog or whatever it is."

"Take my hand," said Belle, her hand reached out to Benji. "I don't want either of us to lose each other in this fog. Especially when it's as busy as it is."

Belle and Benji navigated their way through the crowd as best they could, asking passers-by if they knew where they might find The Three Flapping Ducks, some not knowing at all, others giving them vague directions to streets that seemed far away. As they walked around, Belle paused as she saw a silhouette of a person off in the distance that she thought might be Adam.

"What is it?" asked Benji.

"Nothing. I just—I just thought I saw someone."

"It doesn't matter. Let's keep looking for Kevin," said Belle, as she pulled Benji onwards.

As they kept walking, the fog became thinner and thinner.

"Well, I guess we don't need to hold hands anymore, given how light it is," said Benji.

Eventually, Benji spotted something that looked like three wooden flapping ducks above a building entrance. "Belle, look. I think that's it."

"Finally!"

The girls went inside, explained where they were from, and asked the barkeep if he knew Kevin and where to find him if he did.

"Ah, you'll be them two lasses that insist on serving him tea from time to time."

"Yeah, that's us," Belle said.

"Tea he doesn't particularly care for, mind."

For a moment, shocked at hearing this, it was as if time stood still for both Benji and Belle.

"You mean—" began Belle.

"Aye. He's not one for the taste of the particular type of tea that you girls keep serving him, whatever type of tea that is, I'm not sure, but he don't be likin' it one bit."

Belle and Benji looked at each other, both clearly disheartened.

"Come on, Benji. Let's get out of here."

"Hey," said Belle as they exited, and she looked around, "this isn't where we were before, is it?"

"No, it's okay, Belle. Cities can be like that. Cities aren't like the village at all."

"But the streets are different, I'm sure of it."

"The lighting was different when we came in, and it's sunnier than before, so the way the shadows fall make things look different to how they might have looked when it was foggy or overcast."

"Huh. I guess so. I mean, I never thought of it like that."

"Hey."

"What?"

"Is that a vending machine?"

Belle looked across the street. "Yeah, so?"

"It reminds me of the one at the old, abandoned train station."

"They're pretty common in the city, though, right?"

"I guess so. Let's go have a look anyway."

"Okay."

The girls headed over the road and were particularly intrigued to see this one had a small digital sign on it above the coin slot, which read, "Your destiny awaits. Please insert coins to buy a drink and reveal your destiny."

They thought it was amusing, and Benji encouraged Belle to put in some coins to see what their destiny was. Neither girl could've been more surprised when the red can that Belle picked up from it read "Adam" on the side.

"Do you think he could be here somewhere?" asked Belle.

"Is that who you thought you saw before when you stopped suddenly?"

"Actually, yeah."

"Do you want to try and find him?"

Belle paused for a moment, as her eyes darted around as if looking for answer inside her head. "Honestly, I think it'd be more effort than it's worth. He might come back to the village one day, he might not. Only time will tell."

"Yeah. Come on, let's head home."

"Yeah."

Now back at the ferry, the particularly nice ferryman told the two girls that he was glad to see them heading back, as some bad weather was on its way.

Wide eyed, furrowed brows, and mouths agape, the two girls looked at each other before Belle reported to the ferryman "But there's already been quite a bad storm recently."

"Yeah," added Benji. "It completely decimated the village and everything."

"Don't worry, girls. It's not a Johnathon Storms level event. It's some particularly bad weather."

"You know about Johnathan Storms?" asked Benji.

"Everyone in the local area knows about the Storms."

Benji and Belle found an undercover spot on the ferry, and bad weather did indeed begin to stir up, just as the ferryman had suggested.

To settle their nerves a little, they decided to go and have dinner with Grandma and Grandpa. After they'd spoken about their day, Grandpa said, "So, I guess it feels pretty nice to be back in the correct book. Am I right?" He winked.

Learning to Drive

A few days later, though the weather had been slowly improving here and there, it was raining a little, but not a cause for concern.

Belle had just finished with a late breakfast at Grandma and Grandpa's house, and Grandpa couldn't help but notice Belle eyeing his old car in the backyard through the kitchen window.

"So, I see you've got your eye on the old, uh, horseless carriage, there, Belle?"

"Huh?" said Belle, as if woken from a daydream. "No, I was just looking out the window at your car, thinking about some things."

"Oh, you don't say," said Grandpa, playing along. "And, uh, what are you thinking?"

"If I knew how to drive it, I could go much further than just into the city or into the next town over, in a lot less time than it would take me to walk there. I feel like I could get so much more done in so much less time."

Grandpa, with a raised eyebrow, looked over at Grandma, who was busy doing the dishes.

"Well," said Grandma as she looked back with a small, tense smile and wide eyes.

"Would you like me teach you?" asked Grandpa.

Belle continued to stare blankly out the window, having not quite processed Grandpa's request. She looked over to Grandpa. Both he and Grandma looked at her as if expecting an answer. In a moment's realisation, her eyes widened, and she pointed to herself. "Me? You'll teach me to drive?"

Grandpa slapped his leg and laughed. "Sure. It'll be no trouble. A smart girl like you will pick it up in no time. Once you're all learned up, I'd be happy to let you borrow it whenever need be."

"When can I learn?"

"Now's as good a time as any."

"You two have fun," said Grandma.

After Grandpa's explanations, Belle started up the car and cautiously drove a few metres forward. "Ah! I did it. We're moving! It's so exciting."

Grandpa laughed. "Don't get ahead of yourself. We only moved, what, five metres, if that," Grandpa said as he looked behind the car to see how far they'd moved. "Now you have to put it in reverse and take it back to where we started. *Exactly* where we started. You can tell by the imprints of the wheels in the ground behind us."

Belle leaned out her side of the car and looked back to see where Grandpa was talking about and acknowledged that she could see the imprints.

"Okay, let's go. Ready, Grandpa?"

"Ready when you are."

Belle, leaning out the car and turned to look behind her, carefully drove the car backwards to its original parking spot.

"I did it!" she announced as she emphatically slapped the side of the car.

Grandpa decided to get out of the car and have a look for himself, and while he noticed it wasn't *quite* perfect, he didn't want to take away from Belle's triumph, so rather than criticising her shortcomings, he simply said, "Not bad, Belle. Not bad at all."

"I parked it back perfectly, huh, Grandpa?"

"You did good, kid. You did good. I'd give that a solid eight point five, maybe nine out of ten."

"Nine? Did I not return it perfectly to its previous location?" she said, an eyebrow raised.

"Old Grandpa here's a harsh maker is what it is, Belle!" shouted Grandma from inside the house.

"Old? Who are you callin' old?"

"So, how well did she *really* do?"

"You know what?" said Grandpa. "I think she's ready for the train station."

Belle giggled. "Why would I want to drive to the old train station? I can walk that far."

"Oh no, not the *old* train station. *The* train station. The same one I picked you up from during that storm. The same one where Adam would've come from when he first came here."

Belle's face went blank as her thoughts returned to those times before realising how pleasant of a drive that distance would be. Her eyes lit up like lightbulbs. "You'll really let me drive all the way to the train station and back again?"

"Whoa, slow down there for a minute, Belle. *I'll* drive us both there, and I'll let you drive us back. If you do okay, I might even let you take me into the city one day with *me* as your *guide*. Coming back from the train station is mostly just following road, which actually doesn't teach you anything at all. There's so much more to driving a car than just following a road, and the sooner you learn those intricacies, the better. Get good enough soon enough, and we might just have to look at letting you have your own set of keys."

"My *own* set of keys? You mean you'd let me—"

"Well, hold on there. I have a question for you. What's your *real* reason for wanting to learn to drive? I mean, you mentioned already about travelling further in less time, and that's true, but I can't help but get the feeling your reasons for wanting to drive are more specific than that."

Belle's shoulders slumped, her gaze turned downward, she half folded her arms, and lightly kicked the dirt in front of her.

Grandpa looked over to Grandma, who was looking out the window. With an open hand and a stern yet kind-hearted and sincere look on her face, she gestured towards Belle.

"Oh, come on, Belle. You can tell me. Is it—" he began, looking back to Grandma, who again gestured as she just had. "Is it about Donna or Adam?"

"Both, actually. I haven't heard anything about either of them one way or the other, so I thought if I learnt to drive, I could travel to the village far from the next town over, and from the city to the next city over, to the next city over far beyond where the horizon lies."

Grandma had come out now and was standing next to Grandpa. "Even with a car, that's a long way to travel, Belle."

Grandpa sighed, looked at Grandma, and ran his right hand over the back of his head. "If you do okay with this trip back from the train station, I'll let have the car for the rest of the day, but *only* to travel no further than the village far from the next town over, and *no* further. You're back by dinnertime. Understood?"

"Understood, Grandpa," said Belle with a smile.

"As for the city far beyond the horizon, I've got some old bus tickets."

Grandma's eyes widened, and her brow furrowed "Those old bus tickets? You still have those? Don't you *dare* give Belle those old bus tickets under *any* circumstances."

"Okay, okay," said Grandpa, his hands raised as if afraid of being shot. "I won't."

"You know *darn well* what happened the last time you gave someone those bus tickets," whispered Grandma.

"I know," started Grandpa, his back now turned to Belle, "but I really think Belle's one of the few people who could handle it." His hands now gestured towards Belle.

"Is everything okay? What's wrong with the bus tickets?" interrupted Belle.

"Oh, it's okay, dear," replied Grandma as she scornfully eyed Grandpa. "It's just that I couldn't stand the thought of a nice, young girl like you so far away from the village on her own. If anything were to happen to you, gosh. I don't know what I'd do with myself, especially with everything else that's gone on here lately. Anyway, you never mind about me. You and Grandpa go and have a nice morning's drive, and once you've got the car to yourself, *no further* than the village far from the next town over, okay?"

Belle seemed a little taken aback by Grandma's unexpected sternness, given that she was usually so easy-going, or so Belle always thought. "Okay, Grandma."

"You know what? I *am* gonna let you drive to the train station and back again."

"What? Really?"

"Yep. I'll drive her out right now, you take Grandma back inside, and I'll meet you out the front."

And so, it was done. Belle drove to the train station, went inside, bought a snack and a drink from one of the vending machines, returned to the car, and happily drove all the way back to the village, all the while engaged in idle chit-chat with Grandpa.

But Not Forgotten

Her face wet from tears, Angela had finished making Jacob's bed after having tidied up his room.

"There, that should do it," she said as she got up and brushed herself off, looking around the room at Jacob's old belongings and briefly thinking back on the fond memories related to those items. She headed downstairs and outside and was surprised to see Amanda waiting at the front door, just about ready to knock.

"Oh, Amanda. What are you doing here?"

"I just came to see if everything was okay. How are you doing? I brought snacks," she said as she pointed to the picnic basket hanging on her right arm.

"Oh, thank you. I'm *a lot* better, actually. I just finished," she said, not sure if she could continue speaking, knowing she'd get choked up if she did. "I just finished, um, tidying up Jacob's bedroom and making his bed."

"Oh, that's great. I'm sure he'd would've appreciated that."

"Oh, I'm not so sure," she said, fighting back tears. "He was right at that age where he hated me going into his room."

Amanda smiled, and after a short, awkward silence between them, she asked Angela if she'd like to join her for a walk.

"Actually, if you don't mind, I'd like to stop by Grandpa's place first, but you're welcome to come with me, and we'll go for a walk after that."

"Um, okay. Sure. I mean, if I'm not being any trouble that is."

"Oh, heavens no. It'll be short stop, then we can go.

A bit later, Angela knocked on Grandpa's door.

"Hello, ladies."

"Dad, I'd like to apologize how I've been acting lately in regard to Jacob's passing. I really don't know what came over me, and there's not really any way I can apologise to Adam unless he somehow comes back."

"As for Jacob, we all handle these kinds of things differently. Each person in their own way, and there's no way of knowing how we, or another person, is going to act until it happens. We can imagine what it might be like and how we might react, but until it *actually* happens and is actually there, right in front of us, there's no way of truly knowing how we'll react. As for Adam, he's gone. Don't worry about it."

"I think there's people who need apologizing to more than Adam," said Amanda scornfully, her eyes turned away from both Grandpa and Angela.

Her hand on her chest, Angela wasn't sure what to say next. "I mean, is it something—I mean, I know what I said and what I did, but *other* than that, is there something I should know about?"

"Ugh." Grandpa sighed. "Ever oblivious to the obvious, aren't you, Angela?"

"What?" said Angela, confused, looking back and forth between Grandpa and Amanda.

"Are you kidding me?" asked Grandpa. "Those two always arriving 'fashionably late' and always leaving suspiciously early from almost every social gathering," finished Grandpa with a raised eyebrow, looking at Angela, waiting for the penny to drop.

"Wait, you don't mean—"

"Yes, Angela," added Amanda. "We were basically a couple."

"Oh, Amanda, I'm so sorry. I guess ... I mean ... I don't suppose we could go looking for him?"

"I don't think there's any point," replied Amanda. "When he left, he left. I went to his house to see if everything was all right. We had a brief chat, then I went to the kitchen to make some tea, and when I called to him that it was ready, I got no answer. I checked around the house, and he'd gone, almost as if he was never there."

"Guys," said Grandpa.

"Girls," answered Angela and Amanda simultaneously.

"Guys, girls. Whatever. Belle's borrowed my car in hopes of finding word of Donna in the village far from the next town over, and you never know, whether she finds Donna or not, she may just well find Adam."

"If she'd let me know," said Amanda, "I could've gone with her."

"If he comes back, he comes back. If he doesn't, he doesn't. But I wouldn't get my hopes up. I've lived in this town long enough to know that basically when someone leaves, they leave for good. I don't think there's been anyone in the whole history of this village who's ever come back once they left. Well, maybe one," he said with a wink. "Anyway, you two kids go off and enjoy your picnic."

The two of them excused themselves and left.

Amanda and Angela were now at the picnic bench by the river; Amanda put down her picnic basket.

"Oh, no, not here, Amanda."

"Oh, is everything okay?"

"It's just that here is a little difficult for me right now. This is where everyone was when the storm began and the last place I saw my Jacob."

"Oh. So where do you suggest we go, then?"

"There's a nice eating spot atop a hill just past the next town over where Jacob often mentioned he sat and talked with Sabrina. I never went there before because that was *his* place, and I wanted to allow him his space. And I thought it might be nice to go there. He always spoke of it so fondly. I thought it might be nice to go there."

"Huh. Okay, sure," said Amanda as she picked up the picnic basket. "Let's go."

"So, I believe we can go there directly through the village, but then there's one or two villagers over there, and if we bump into them, we'll be there for the rest of day chatting. Or we can go around. As I understand it, it takes a little longer, but it's not as steep and is *far* more scenic."

"Let's go that way."

"Agreed."

"Oh gosh, my legs," said Amanda as she and Angela emerged from the forest heading towards the hill.

"Tell me about it," replied Angela. "Oh look, someone carved their initials into the tree in a love heart. How sweet," she said with a smile. "I wonder who it is," she continued as she wandered over to the tree. "Oh my!"

"What is it?" asked Amanda as she hurried over. "Oh!" she giggled.

"J.H. plus S.B."

Amanda couldn't help but giggle.

"Amanda, this is serious. Do you know what this means?"

"Oh, I know *exactly* what that means."

"But my sweet innocent little boy."

"Sweet? Yes. Innocent? Apparently not so much. Or at least not as much as you thought," she said, continuing to giggle.

"Oh, Amanda."

"Oh, come on. How is this not that cutest thing *ever*?"

"Clearly we don't see eye to eye on this matter."

"Clearly not."

"That Sabrina—"

"Whoa! No!" began Amanda, becoming suddenly serious. "Seriously. No. You have no certainty whose idea it was in the first place, or whether or not it was a mutual decision, so you have no right to judge."

"Regardless, I'm still a little shocked by this."

"Don't worry about it. It is what it is, and I think it's cute. Come on, sit down and let's have our picnic."

The two of the sat down and prepared the picnic. Angela noticed that Amanda had some of Donna's father's famous cordial and asked her if she knew how Donna's parents were handling the loss.

"Honestly, I don't know. I haven't checked in on them. Belle would probably be the best person to ask about that."

"Understood. I always feel like I should toast to something when I have this cordial."

"What would you like to toast to?"

"To new beginnings and fresh starts."

"To young love," replied Amanda as she smiled and pointed to the carved initials on the tree, "fresh starts and new beginnings."

"Oh, Amanda," sneered Angela lightly.

Amanda giggled.

"Okay, fine. For Jacob's sake."

"For Jacob's sake."

"To young love, fresh starts, and new beginnings."

They clinked their glasses together, drank their cordial, continued in idle conversation, and enjoyed what was left of the midday sun.

Black Velvet

I t was a little past breakfast, and Belle was headed out for a walk when she spotted a parcel placed at the doorstep.

"Ah!" she squealed. "It's finally here."

"What is it, dear?" called her mother from the kitchen.

"My chauffeur uniform I ordered from the catalogue the other day."

Belle picked up the package, closed the door, and sat down in the living room, a smile beaming across her face from ear to ear. She excitedly, hastily, and somewhat aggressively opened the package. She put the driver's cap and goggles to one side, and as she removed the clothes and held them up, her eyeballs widened considerably.

"Oh no, dear," said her mother, looking on in horror from the kitchen. "Those are men's clothes."

"Yeah, I know," said Belle hastily, dismissing her mother's comment. "And isn't it *beautiful*?"

The uniform, which Belle couldn't take her eyes off, along with the aforementioned driver's cap and goggles, was a black velvet, gold-buttoned, double-breasted long-sleeve jacket, a pair of relaxed-fit loose leather pants, knee-high boots, and dainty, also leather, driving gloves.

Belle froze with excitement and could take neither her eyes nor her hands off her new outfit.

"Well, Belle," said her mother, "you know I'm not particularly fond of this tomboyish side that you have, and I likely never will be. However, if what you ordered is what you ordered and that's what you're happy with, then so be it."

"It's my outfit, Mum. I paid for it with my own money."

"Well, again, so be it, but aren't you at least going to try it on?"

Belle was so mesmerized by her outfit combined with the thought of wearing it as she drove from town to town, she only heard that her mother had spoken but not what she'd said.

"This outfit is amazing. I'm gonna go upstairs and try it on."

After a decent amount of time, Belle came back down the stairs, and her mother was quite surprised to see, even though they were men's clothes, just how womanly Belle looked in them. "How do they fit, dear?"

"Honestly, they're just a *little* too tight, but it's not a dealbreaker or anything. Other than that, they're quite comfortable."

"Well, you could always return them."

"I'm not returning them. I remember looking at the catalogue, and the next size up would've been too loose fitting for me. I'm actually okay with this size."

"Are you going to complete the uniform?" asked Belle's mother as she gestured towards the driver's cap and goggles on the coffee table.

"Oh, gosh, I forgot them in my excitement. How did I remember the gloves but forget the cap and goggles?" She laughed.

"I guess you've always been a little bit like that, haven't you?"

She giggled. "I guess I have."

Distant from Home, but Nearer to Thee

As Adam trudged through unfamiliar terrain, he pulled his trench coat tighter around him. He saw few stars twinkle through the constant downpour, hidden not only by the clouds, but also by the high treetops. He looked up and around, uncertain of where he was, his only saving grace the rainclouds emphasising the brightness of the full moon.

The tears streaming down his face hidden by the relentless rainfall, he looked around for any sign of civilization—a streetlamp, a road sign, the sound of a boat or train in the distance—but heard and saw nothing. The wind getting stronger, he held his hat to his head and kept walking with a strange feeling of familiarity and strangeness at the same time, almost as if he was simultaneously coming and going, but he knew not from where nor where to.

Suddenly, he bumped into a lone tree. "Sorry!"

"Oh, sorry. I thought maybe you were a person," he said before he noticed something carved into the tree in the shape of a love heart. "J ... H ... S ... B. Jay ... Ess ... I know those initials. Jacob and Sabrina," he said as he turned from side to side, looking for signs of life. "Where's the village? Shouldn't somebody have their lights on? It can't be far. I guess I'll just keep going."

And keep going he did, fumbling through unbeaten paths and untrodden bushland, still holding on to his hat, and pulling his trench coat as tight around him as he could.

The rain got heavier, the wind blew harder, and somehow even the sky grew darker. He stopped.

"Please," he said, falling to his knees, clasping his hands together. "If there is *anyone*, any*thing*, *any* kind of Greater Power whatsoever in this cold world, I ..." He paused as he thought of what he wanted to ask. "I don't even know what I'm trying to ask or if this is even what praying is. I just ..." He paused again, this time really concentrating on what he wanted to say. "I just need a little help."

Unexpectedly, he was overcome with a warmth he'd never felt before, a feeling of weightlessness washing over him, and without having realised he was standing again. The rain had stopped, the wind died down, and the clouds had parted. Before him was a glowing white silhouette, about the size and shape of a boy.

"Jacob?" he asked.

The figure slowly glided away from Adam, down the unbeaten, moonlit path, and eventually faded back into nothing.

"Right. I guess I should go that way, then."

Adam walked and walked and walked, following the moonlit path, his legs sore after so much walking.

"I need somewhere to sit down," he said, and much to his surprise, as soon as he'd said it, something lit up in the distance and buzzed in the way that only certain electric lights can. As Adam came closer and closer, he couldn't quite believe his eyes. "It's not, is it?"

He walked onwards, spurred on by the enthusiasm of what he thought the light couldn't possibly be.

"It is," he said as he approached ever nearer.

"It's the vending machine," he said in total and utter disbelief. "It can't be, and yet there it is."

He looked back, thinking that he definitely didn't pass the Inconvenience Store, and yet he must have, although he was certain he hadn't. Looking around the old train station, he marvelled at the repair job. What was once dilapidated, falling apart, and in a horrid state of disrepair was now almost as if it were brand new.

"It doesn't quite look like it used to, but by gosh, there's no way that this isn't the old train station. And the vending machine."

He marvelled at the brand-new vending machine, knowing full well that it hadn't been replaced, but somehow, of its own accord, renewed.

Adam stepped slightly out of the train station, looking towards the village, and thought that the middle of the night probably wasn't the best time to return, so he took shelter in the train station, resting on one of its benches. "Compared to what I've been through this past week or so, this is basically the Ritz."

Adam made himself as comfortable as could be, thankful for the shelter from the weather, and as best he could, drifted slowly, although uncomfortably, off to sleep.

Farewell, Most Beautiful

Just past the crack of dawn earlier that same day, Belle had already arisen, eaten her breakfast, put on her chauffeur's uniform and was ready to face the day. She grabbed her duffel bag, which she'd fully packed the night before, headed out her front door, and made her way over to see Grandpa.

"Hello, Grandpa," she said as he approached him, as he was working in his front garden.

He turned around, and seeing Belle, stopped what he was doing, stood up and greeted her. "Well, don't *you* look the part," he said in acknowledgement of her outfit.

"Yeah. I wanted to look as authentic as possible."

"Well, I can't disagree. You definitely look like you're ready to go off on an adventure, and judging by that duffel bag, it looks like you're planning to be gone for a while."

"That's exactly what I've come to talk to you about."

Grandma came out from the house to the front porch, sipping on her first cup of tea for the day. She looked at the way Belle was dressed and how she was packed, then looked to Grandpa, the two of them sharing an acknowledging glance.

"We know why you've stopped by, Belle. And it's not just to borrow the car, is it?"

"Uh, about that," replied Belle. "I was kind of wondering if—"

"Stop right there, Belle. It's yours."

"Oh, you," said Grandma as she smiled and rolled her eyes. "You never could resist a beautiful lady, could you?"

"Well, I'm still here with you, aren't I?" he said.

"Oh, stop it."

"You two are so cute sometimes." Belle giggled, which embarrassed both Grandma and Grandpa.

"Anyway," said Grandpa, "here are the keys." He pulled the keys out of his coat's inner top-left pocket.

"Oh, thank you," replied Belle as she graciously accepted them.

"The car is right there in driveway, ready to go. Pointed in the right direction and everything," said Grandpa as he started choking up a little.

"This village is going to miss you, Belle," said Grandma. "It's going to miss you so much. The village and all of the people in it."

"Thank you, Grandma. Over the past few days, I've said my goodbyes to everyone I need to say goodbye to. And what with everything that's been going on lately, I tried to do it with as little fuss and bother as possible. Everyone knows I'm leaving today, and I won't come back until I've found what I'm looking for."

"Just remember, dear," began Grandma, "what we're looking for isn't always what we think it is. Sometimes it is, and sometimes it turns out to be something *completely* different."

"And sometimes it's both," added Grandpa.

Belle furrowed her brow and tilted her head as her eyes darted around, looking for the meaning of what she just heard, and finally replying with a simple, "Yeah."

"Well, I guess we'll be seein' ya," said Grandpa as he walked Belle over and helped her put her things in the car.

Belle got in the car, started the engine, and as tears welled in her eyes, waved, and with a very firm and acknowledging nod, silently said goodbye.

"So many people leave this village," said Grandma.

"And so few ever come back," replied Grandpa.

Repairing the Past

It was long after breakfast and nowhere near lunchtime. The village was alive with the hustle and bustle of all the tradesfolk who had come to help repair after the recent spell of bad weather.

Max wandered along the main road, observing all the builders help restore the village.

"Max," Grandpa called out with a smile, "get over here"

"Oh, Grandpa," said Max as he walked over to Grandpa. "I was just wondering if I could help with anything."

"Let me tell you right now, kid, sometimes the best thing you can do to help in these kinds of situations is just stay out of everyone's way."

"As true as that is," came the sound of an unfamiliar voice, "we could actually use an extra pair of hands over by the few houses next to the Town Dinner Hall."

"And you are?" asked Grandpa.

"Name's Aloysius, but everyone calls me Al."

"Whew, they sure don't make 'em like they make you, do they?" said Grandpa as reached up to shake Al's hand.

"No, they don't," replied Al as he smiled and crouched down slightly to shake Grandpa's hand. Grandpa winced as they shook.

"This here is Max," said Grandpa as he rubbed his now-free hand. "If you need an extra pair of hands, Max here is as good as any."

"I mean, that's fine," replied Max. "I don't mind helpin' out none, I just kinda wish Adam was still around, you know?"

"Adam?" asked Al. "I don't know any Adam."

"Looking for someone?" asked Adam, having had appeared from behind Al.

"Adam!" said both Max and Grandpa with beaming smiles.

"Oh, so this is Adam," said Al. "If it's all the same to you fellas, I guess I'll get back to work."

"Not a problem," said Grandpa.

"I'll join you," said Max.

"We didn't think you'd come back," said Grandpa. "So few people ever do."

"Well, I uh, guess that makes me one of the exceptions to the rule."

"Oh, ah. *One* of, that's right. There's been the odd one or two here and there who came back."

"Yourself included, from memory."

"Hey, have you seen my wife?" asked Grandpa, his palms open, arms outstretched. "You know that beautiful young lady that everyone around here calls Grandma? She's why I came back."

"Ah, what can I say, Grandpa?" replied Adam, his left hand on his hip, while his right hand gestured towards the village. "This town *does* have its fair share of beautiful women."

"Speaking of beautiful women, you still remember where Amanda lives, right?"

"I do. But I'd rather help out with the reconstruction efforts for the time being. I've got plenty of time to see Amanda afterwards," said Adam with a dismissive wave of his right hand.

"Oh, plenty of time?"

"Plenty," he replied with his arms out and his palms down in an attempt to prevent Grandpa from saying any more.

"Huh. I am glad to hear that, and so will she be."

"Oh, and you'll be glad to know there's a certain someone else who's come back to help with the reconstruction efforts."

Grandpa raised an eyebrow.

"A certain freckle-faced someone with very mysterious green eyes."

"Joshua's here too?" asked Grandpa as he pointed to the reconstruction efforts.

"He is. He's down near the Town Dinner Hall."

"Well, I can't wait to see that old son of a gun again."

"In fact," began Adam as he placed his right hand on Grandpa's left shoulder and turned to start walking to the Town Dinner Hall, "he's part of the reason I came back. It's a long, *long* story, but I'm sure I'll have time to tell it to you one day."

"Boy, oh boy. Joshua, back in the village. You know he's one of the few that I thought when they left, he'd be gone for good."

"There's just something about this old town, isn't there?"

"There sure is, Adam, there sure is."

The Town Dinner Hall was as busy as busy could be with tradesfolk sitting everywhere, eating. Angela and Amanda were amongst the few serving the food. Adam walked up to the serving area, grabbed a tray, and stood in line behind the others. Adam tried to strike up a conversation with Amanda as she served him, but her expression was plain, and her words directly related to the food he'd like to order, offering only short, sharp answers to any other type of questions he asked. Finally, she told him the price of what he ordered and put out her hand.

"Huh," he began, as he reached in his pockets to gather the money to pay, "so that's how it is."

"You don't get to come back here and start talking to me like nothing happened. Now pay up."

"Understood," he said as he handed over the necessary cash, walked off, and found somewhere to sit.

About halfway through his meal, Adam heard an all-too-familiar voice ask if she could sit with him. "Oh, Angela. By all means, please. It'll be nice to have some company."

Her voice shaking and uncertain of her words, Angela tried her best to apologise for her actions on the night of the storm.

"It's fine," said Adam. "I can only imagine what it must've been like for you at that time."

"I only saw what I saw, whereas you saw it happen with your own eyes. You and Sabrina."

"Oh, how is Sabrina?"

"She's handled it *so* well. I don't know how she's done it, but she has. When I talk to her these days, she seems, how do I put this? She seems well, but somehow distant. Lost in thoughts about Jacob, I suppose."

"Speaking of Jacob, have you given him a proper farewell?"

"We haven't. Not yet. We're waiting for the village to be rebuilt. It took me a long time to come to terms with his passing, but I think you're right. Giving him a proper funeral would help, I think."

"Believe me," said Adam with a distant look on his face, "it would."

"Is everything all right?"

"I, um, I've been to my fair share of funerals, and believe me, it definitely helps. Every single time, without fail, having a funeral is *definitely* the right way to go."

"Oh, Adam, I can only imagine what your life must have been like before you came here."

"It was, um ... let's just say I'm glad I found this place, and I'm glad I came back," he said as he looked over at Amanda. Angela turned her head to see what he was looking at. "Oh, Amanda," said Angela as she placed her right hand on Adam's left forearm. "She'll come around."

"Anyway," he said as he wiped his face clean and picked up the tray, ready to return it, "there's work to be done."

"Don't worry about the tray," said Angela as she reached for it. "I'll take care of that."

"Are you sure?"

"It's *literally* my job."

"Oh, thank you. Then I'll get on with helping these fine folk rebuild this fine village."

And that he did.

Getting to Know You Better

A few days had passed, and with Adam's help, the village had been rebuilt considerably faster than expected. Of course, the clear weather also helped.

Adam had settled back into the house at the edge of the village nicely, almost as if it was his own home, and just as he'd settled into the main chair in the living room, someone knocked.

"Knock, knock," called Amanda as she rapped on the front door of the house.

Surprised, Adam immediately rose from his chair to go and answer the door. "Amanda. To what do I owe the pleasure?" he said awkwardly.

"And Angela," replied Amanda as she gestured to Angela, who was standing a few feet back, on the stairs that led up to the veranda. "We were just wondering," began Amanda, as she had her arms beside her, then in front of her, then behind her, "if you wanted to join us," she continued, her gaze almost anywhere except in direct contact with Adam's.

Angela raised her arm, drawing attention to the picnic basket she was carrying. "I thought we might go and sit by the river."

"Actually, there's a location just towards the back of the village I noticed when I first came here that looks like an overgrown old playground. I thought that might be a nice area if it were cleaned up a little first."

"You're right," said Angela, "*if* it were cleaned up first, but for now, as you've said, it's overgrown. I really think the river is the best place for now."

"Right you are. The river it is."

At that one particular picnic table by the river, Angela and Amanda sat next to each other and Adam across from Angela, his back to the river. After far too long of an awkward silence, Angela decided to say something. "So, you must have been on quite an adventure between leaving and coming back."

Adam took a deep breath as his eyes glazed over. His mind was taken back to not only the night of the storm and the night he returned, but also how truly lost he was between those two nights. Lost not only of his location but also of heart and mind.

"Adam?" said Amanda. "Are you okay?"

"Huh?" he said, as he snapped back to the moment. "Oh, yeah. I'm fine. It, um, it was quite an adventure, Angela."

"Based on the look on your face just now, it was quite an ordeal. I don't mean to pry, but would you mind telling us about it?"

"Angela!" interrupted Amanda. "Oh," she began, looking at Adam, "she doesn't *mean* to pry, but somehow that's what she's doing."

Angela frowned, looked down, and sighed. "No, I really don't *mean* to pry. It's just that I'm hoping to get a clear picture of what you went through. I feel so responsible for—I *do* feel responsible for you having left the village on that night. So,

I'm just looking for a clearer picture of *exactly* what I was responsible for."

"Oh, so you're making it about *you*? Is that it?" asked Amanda.

"*No*. Well, yes, but ... Amanda, *please*. Maybe I'm not the best communicator in the world, but you don't know what's in my mind and my heart, and words are the only way I have of communicating those things. So please, let me just—I don't even know anymore," she said as she rested her face in her hands.

"No, Amanda," began Adam, "it's quite all right. I honestly don't mind retelling it." He turned to Amanda, with a slight look of scornfulness on his face. "If anything, I appreciate that there's someone willing to listen to me share my experiences with them."

"Oh," said Amanda, as she looked around as if looking for the right thing to say. "I think I'm just gonna go and leave you to it."

"Well, thanks for joining us, and I'll see you again some other time," said Adam.

Once Adam had decided that Amanda was a decent distance from himself and Angela, he began telling her the tale of his adventures.

"The things I'm about to tell you, Angela, I warn you, are *quite* something to be told and are not for the faint of heart. It may even seem like a tall tale, but I assure you, every word of it is true."

"Believe me, Adam, it can't *possibly* be any more unusual than any of the adventures Jacob and Sabrina used to tell me about."

"Right. Well then, here we go."

Adam took a deep breath and relayed the tale of his adventure.

Musings

With Adam and Angela behind her at that one particular picnic table by the river, Amanda wandered home, her gaze downwards, her hands clasped behind her, her shoulders slouched, her feet kicking the occasional rock here and there. She wondered about what they might talk about, and she thought back on what life was like before the recent horrendous storm.

A gentle breeze blew a leaf to her feet, which reminded her of how Jacob used to collect them and add them to his pressed-leaf collection, which made her think about how much Sabrina must be missing Jacob, which in turn made her wonder how many more people were lost in that storm, which brought her mind to how Belle must have felt, knowing Donna got swept away by the river with hope that, somewhere out there, she was still alive.

"Hence why she borrowed Grandpa's car to go looking for her," said Sabrina.

"Oh, Sabrina," said Amanda, startled. "Where did ...? How did ...?"

"Max said he saw you, Adam, and Angela heading out this way, so we thought we'd come over and say hi. That, and you were mumbling to yourself just as I was passing by."

Amanda laughed. "I didn't even realise I was doing that."

"Yeah, I got the feeling," said Benji.

"Benji. You're here too?"

"I walk a little faster than Sabrina, so by the time you'd both stopped, I was standing behind you."

"You *do* have this knack for seeming to appear as if out of nowhere."

Benji smiled. "It's just how I am, I guess."

"Anyway, I think I'm just gonna head on back to the village. I think Adam's telling Amanda about what happened to him while he was gone."

"Oh, I love hearing those kinds of stories," said Benji.

"Jacob used to have so many of those," began Sabrina, "especially from when he came back from wondering off by himself."

"I loved hearing those." Benji smiled. "Some of those tales were *quite* tall."

Were they, though? thought Sabrina. Through the bushes, she eyed the vending machine at the old train station, her mind thinking back on her recent visit to the big train station and the vending machine she came across halfway there that wasn't there when she walked back.

"Anyway, come on, Sabrina," said Benji as she took Sabrina's arm. "I wanna hear about what happened to Adam. I hope we haven't missed any of the good bits."

"See you, Amanda," said Sabrina as she was dragged off by Benji.

Amanda bid them good day and continued back to the village.

Recounting That Night's Events

Adam was about to start telling Angela what happened to him on the night of the storm, just as Sabrina and Benji arrived at the table.

"Do you mind if you we join you?' asked Benji.

"By all means, please join us," asked Adam.

"So, it was the night of the storm," began Adam. "I was at home packing and looking quite forward to the tea that Amanda had just offered to make me."

Adam had gone to his room to pack more of his clothes when a flash of lightning followed very closely by a monstrously loud clap of thunder scared the living daylights out of him.

Suddenly, Adam was no longer in his room, but outside amongst the trees, getting wet in the pouring rain. He quickly turned around from one direction to another, shocked at what had happened.

"Amanda?" he called out. "Hello? Anyone?"

He saw a light off in the distance in what appeared to be a small building with some people inside, so headed in that direction.

That's the old train station, thought Adam. *Who's inside, I wonder?*

And with that Adam suddenly found himself inside the train station, impartially observing the events of only an hour or so before. He was watching himself and Sabrina move the vending machine off of Jacob's corpse.

He stood there silently watching, knowing he couldn't interact or interfere with the events, wondering why he was being shown this at all.

After witnessing Sabrina and himself leave the train station with the corpse, he was perplexed to see what looked like an apparition of Jacob rise from the floor as if getting up from a bad fall.

"What happened?" the boy asked.

"Jacob?" asked Adam.

"Yes? Oh, it's you," said Jacob's ghost. "I'm supposed to tell you something before I go."

"Tell me something? Tell me what?"

"Oh that's, right," said Jacob. "There are no accidents," he finished, his voice sounding ethereal.

"Right," replied Adam, confused.

And with that, Jacob's ghost was engulfed in an incredible white light, and Adam suddenly found himself upon a hilltop not far from the village, dry as a bone, as the sun rose in the east and gave the land a warm orange glow.

Adam looked around again, seeing a picnic table, on it a lone glass of red wine next to a bottle.

"Hello?" he said as he approached the table, although no answer came. He sat at the table and looked at the label on the wine. "Joshua's Miracle? I wonder who Joshua is?"

"I am," said Joshua, sitting on the other side of the picnic table.

Adam flinched. "Sorry. I didn't realise someone was sitting there."

"There wasn't. Now there is, and here I am. Is there something you'd like to discuss?"

Adam sighed quietly and rested his chin in the palm of his right hand, his gaze landing upon the half-filled glass of red wine. "I don't suppose there is much I'd like to discuss."

"You care not to speak of your banishment from the village?" asked Jacob in a stern tone.

"Ah. You asked me specifically if I would *like* to talk about something, not if I *wanted* to talk about something. Just because a person *wants* to talk about something doesn't necessarily mean they're going to like it."

"Huh," replied Joshua. "Well, you've got me on that one."

The scenery once again changed around Adam, as he now found himself seated at an almost entirely unfamiliar train station as dust blew up all around.

"*Old red*," he thought, as a magnificent looking, burgundy coloured steam train pulled up to the station.

"I remember this place," he said. "It's the train station I first came from that took me to the village in the first place."

"Are you quite all right, sir?" asked an elderly lady.

"You can see me?"

"As well as I can see anyone. Should I not be seeing you?"

"Wait. Let me guess. You've got some kind of seemingly all-important message for me which is ultimately just a vague lesson, poorly disguised."

The woman scoffed. "Troublesome lot. Every last one of you. Here, take this." She reached into her bag and pulled out a ticket that glowed with a molten gold aura. "It might not take you where you *want* to go," she said. "But it will assuredly take you where you *need* to go. Now be off with you," she said dismissively before she boarded the train.

As Adam waited to once again be whisked away to a new location, the dust settled, people boarded and alighted the train, and the elderly lady leaned out the window and shouted, "Well? Are you coming or not?"

"Me?" he said, as he looked around and at his glowing train ticket.

"Yes, you. Fool!"

"Right you are," he said, and hurried aboard the train.

As he boarded the train and looked for a seat, the scenery once again changed around him. Now back at the village, he was witnessing moments before the first time he met Amanda as she was puttering around in the garden. On closer inspection, it seemed she was actually burying an animal. Likely the one she'd told Adam about before that was injured by the bike that remained against the old, abandoned train station.

"I didn't realise that had happened so recently."

An apparition of Amanda, separate from the physical one Adam was witnessing, stood up, looked Adam directly in the eye, and said, "Time isn't always what you think it is."

Adam sighed. "More strange and vague messages."

The scenery changed again, this time to a vibrant and busy city square.

"No, not this," said Adam as he started to tremble. "This is why I headed off to the village in the first place."

Adam now bore witness to an incident on the side of the road, involving a growing number of people crowding around the area. Given how hazy the air was, it was hard to make out quite what was going on.

"I don't want to see this. Please stop showing me these things."

"No."

"Who said that?" said Adam, as he darted around, looking from side to side to where the solitary *no* had come from.

"No, please. *Anything* but *this*."

Adam waited, but nothing changed, so he approached the incident slowly and cautiously. It was a road accident. A young boy had been severely injured. "He looks to be not much older than Jacob, if not the same age."

I remember this, thought Adam as he watched a past version of himself hold the young boy in his arms. "I'd just parked the car, and as I was getting out, the boy came speeding along on his bike and ran headfirst into my door. It killed him instantly."

The boy opened his eyes and looked directly at Adam.

"This isn't, wasn't, never has been, and never shall be your fault. Don't let the ignorance of others convince you that you're the one to blame. It's just something that happened. Neither my fault nor yours. Simply, it is the way of things."

Again, the scenery changed, and Adam was at the factory where he once worked, a sweatshop where men were lifting heavy things and moving them around, while others were banging mallets against steel for any variety of reasons. Machinery was all around, making all sorts of banging and clanging type noises.

"Anywhere but here. This is where the twins Hank and Frank had that hideous accident. I was a wreck for days. I don't want to see this again."

As he looked around, he saw the series of events that led to Hank and Frank's eventual demise.

"No!" he screamed, horrified.

He turned away and ran straight for the exit and out into the pouring rain. "Where am I now?"

He looked around and realised he was simply outside the factory. "I want no part of this." He ran and ran and ran, not paying any attention to whatever scenarios he was shown, eventually in the midst of an unfamiliar forest. He pulled his trench coat tighter around him as he saw few stars twinkle through the constant downpour, hidden not only by the clouds but also by the high treetops. He looked up and around, uncertain of where he was, his only saving grace the rainclouds emphasising the brightness of the full moon. The tears streaming down his face hidden by the relentless rainfall, he looked around for any sign of civilization—a streetlamp, a road sign, the sound of a boat or train in the distance, but heard and saw nothing.

"And that's when I bumped into the tree with Jacob and Sabrina's initials carved into it, up on the hill over there," he said as he pointed to the hill in the distance and finally finished his story.

"Well," began Angela, "that was certainly quite an adventure."

"Oh, wow," said Benji. "I wonder how I can go on such an adventure."

"It sounds exciting, doesn't it? But believe me, it's quite harrowing."

"And I thought Jacob's tales were tall," said Sabrina.

"I don't know what to tell you, Sabrina. That's what happened."

"Anyway," said Sabrina as she stood up, "Benji and I are off to see Kevin."

"All right then. Enjoy yourselves," said Adam.

"Have fun, girls," said Angela.

Benji and Sabrina walked off, and Angela and Adam finished up before they headed back to the village.

Pink Lotus

In a clearing deep in the bushlands, not too far from the hill which lay just beyond the next town over, stood a majestic church, its belfry thrust skywards, although not nearly as high as some of the surrounding trees. Similar to many other areas surrounding the village, it was mysteriously and meticulously well kept, although no one knew who it was that kept it that way. The church was built of brown bricks, adorned with numerous stunning stained-glass windows, each window telling a part of a story from long ago, although perhaps not the story you would expect in a church.

As each of the villagers gazed upon the windows, they were a little spooked by the stained-glass windows' images, which told the tale of the village itself, along with every one of their own lives. Images from when Joshua first arrived, to Jacob and Sabrina's first kiss by the tree on the hill. Even the old train station and the vending machine within it were immortalized in one of the windows.

"Oh," said Angela as if concerned. She very deliberately passed her eyes over each of the images in the window. "The vending machine."

"What about it?" asked Benji, appearing as if from nowhere as she looked at a vending machine beside the entrance to the church.

"Huh?" said Angela, a little startled by Benji's seemingly sudden appearance. "Oh, Benji, it's just you," she said, breathing a sigh of relief. "You really *do* have a habit of sneaking up on people, you know?"

Benji smiled. "I think it's my superpower. Anyway, what were you saying about the vending machine?" asked Benji as she pointed to the vending machine by the church's main entrance.

"It's just that the windows—" said Angela as she pointed to the windows while looking towards where Benji pointed. "There's a vending machine on holy ground?" she said scornfully. "How disrespectful!"

"I think it's okay because it's such a long walk from the village; they probably thought people would be quite parched by the time they got here. That, and it's only got healthy drinks such as water and various juices in it. No soda, sports, or energy drinks, and all the snacks are healthy, such as muesli bars and so on."

"Oh, I suppose you're right. Come to think of it, I am a bit parched," she said as she approached the vending machine to get a drink and asked for forgiveness for using it, not having yet realised that almost everyone there had already purchased a drink from the very same machine.

Benji looked around at who was there and who was yet to arrive and became excited when she saw Sabrina walking up the stairs to the church. As she trotted up the stairs by the other patrons all wearing black, her pink outfit made it look as if she was a pink lotus rising from beneath a black river's surface.

"Hi, Sabrina."

"Hi, Benji. Hi, Mrs. H," replied Sabrina with slight smile and the slightest of bows.

"Pink?" scorned Angela. "And what kind of a colour do you suppose that is to be wearing at a funeral?"

Sabrina turned her eyes upwards for a moment and thought about how to answer. "Pink," she began before a slight pause, "is exactly the colour I think Jacob would've expected me to wear to his funeral."

Angela looked at Sabrina and didn't really know how to respond. She nodded and lowered her head in an attempt to hide her tears. "Fair enough. I guess you knew him better than I did anyway."

"Not at all. How could a girl as young as me possibly know a young boy like Jacob better than his own mother?"

"I suppose we all knew Jacob in different ways," inserted Benji. "Just like he would've known us all in different ways from how we know each other."

"I suppose so." Angela dried her tears. "Shall we?" she said as she gestured towards the church.

The three of them entered the church, took their places next to Adam and Amanda, and the funeral began.

Eventually, Sabrina was summoned to the altar to perform her eulogy, but just a moment before, asked Angela if she had anything she'd like to add.

"No," she whispered. "I read your eulogy last night, and you've said everything I could've possibly wanted to say, and likely said it better too. Please, go on."

Sabrina ascended the stairs to the podium by the altar, and as she rose up the stairs, she strongly felt Jacob's presence in her mind's eye, gently whispering in her ear about her choice of clothing, *"nice,"* and giving her a thumbs-up, which made her smile, although she regained her composure before she turned to face the crowd and stand at the podium.

"Jacob's effervescence was contagious," began Sabrina.

"Why does she always have to use such big words?" whispered Angela to Amanda.

"Because that's just who she is."

The eulogy continued. "... and when we arrived at what Jacob always referred to as the Inconvenience Store, it was like no time had passed at all. Like many present, Jacob was born and raised in the village and loved by all. Always enthusiastic about whatever he set his heart to, he would always welcome newcomers to the village with open arms and an open heart."

As Sabrina said this, her mind went back to when Adam first arrived at the village, and she remembered fondly the warm welcome that Jacob gave him. It was as if he was an old friend returned from a long and arduous journey.

"... and although Jacob may be unable to be with us furthermore," continued Sabrina, "he will live on with us forever, eternal in our hearts. Rest in peace, Jacob, and peace be with you."

"And also with you," replied a few of the congregation.

Celebrating Life

Later that same day, people were back at the village, socializing in the Town Dinner Hall. Angela quietly pulled Sabrina aside. They were standing next to a wall beside the piano near the stage.

"I had no idea you were such a good speaker," said Angela.

"Thank you, Mrs. H."

"Oh, Sabrina, please. While I understand the formality, we've known each other your whole life, so it's perfectly okay to call me Angela."

"Okay," she replied before taking a sip of lemonade.

"But really, I was so moved by your words. They were honestly quite powerful."

Sabrina tilted her head and rubbed one of her arms. "Uh, thanks. Honestly, Angela, I don't really know what to say," she finished, moving her cup up in front of her.

"Have you ever considered a career as a writer?"

"Uh, well. I mean, I like writing at school, but I never really considered making a career of it. It's not like I ever got very good marks for it. I mean, I never got terribly bad marks either, just not very good ones."

"Well, obviously your teachers don't know talent when they see it. Anyway, it's something to consider. I'm going to go and see what Adam and Amanda are up to. Why don't you go and see Belle?"

"Belle's here?"

"She's right over there," said Angela.

Angela approached Adam and noticed Amanda's head was down, her face smiling, and Adam's face was just a little red.

"Well, excuse me." She gasped softly, her hand placed to her chest. "You're not *flirting* at my Jacob's after-funeral, are you?"

Amanda's smile disappeared instantly, her head raised, Adam's face becoming appropriately white.

"Oh, gosh, Angela," began Amanda, "no, not at all."

Adam shook his head.

"You can't pull the wool over my eyes. I know what flirting looks like when I see it."

"You know what?" said Adam. "Perhaps we'll just do the rounds quickly and be on our way."

"As I was *just* about to suggest. Now be on your way."

Sabrina walked up to Belle, who was talking with Benji; they were both enjoying the finger food from the table at which they both stood.

"Hi," said Sabrina.

"Hi," replied Belle happily. "I everything okay? I know you and Jacob were close."

"Uh, yeah. Everything's fine, actually. I sort of said goodbye to him in my own way about a week or so ago, up at the picnic table by the tree on the hill just past the next town over."

"Oh, I know the place."

"Aaand, how about you? Your search for Donna, I mean."

"No luck, I'm afraid. But I did manage to catch up with Kevin and went for a drive into the city and then out into the countryside. Unfortunately, he couldn't make it here today."

"That's okay. I'm sure we'll catch up with him again."

Eating a Late Lunch

Belle and Benji sat on Grandma and Grandpa's front steps. It was getting cooler as the days passed by, and the girls were admiring how the leaves were slowly changing colour from their usual vibrant greens to their autumn browns, reds, and yellows. The sun was far from high in the sky, and nowhere near set, but definitely lower in the sky than it was higher and cast a warm orange glow over the village as the leaves of the trees split the sun's light into God rays.

Belle sat on the porch at the top of the steps as she usually did, with Benji sitting directly next to her.

"I'd feel a bit strange sitting on the same step as Donna used to," began Benji, "especially knowing that you still haven't found her yet. I'm sorry about that, by the way."

"That's okay. A body hasn't been found, so that's a good sign she's still alive out there somewhere."

Benji looked at her feet, then around at the village, upwards to the sky and the trees, and again around the village. "I feel like I wanna have a conversation with you, but I'm just not sure what do say. You know, because—"

"No, it's okay," interrupted Belle. "I understand."

"So, what did you and Donna used to talk about? I mean, if I can ask."

"No, it's fine, really." Belle smiled. "We used to sit here and talk about nothing. Just whatever was on our minds. Usually about what we were eating, though."

"So, what *are* you eating?"

"Some chicken noodle soup along with, as always, last night's spaghetti Bolognese leftovers. And you?"

"See for yourself."

Benji had brought with her a fruit salad that was in a small, round tub and was composed of chunks of watermelon, apple, orange, grape, pawpaw, cantaloupe, and honey melon, every last one of them sweet and moist, dripping with the freshness of the morning dew.

Belle smiled. "That looks incredible," she said, her mind taken back to when Donna would eat exactly the same thing. "It smells good too."

"Not to mention how much better it's made by the soft, milky texture given to it by this yogurt I've added."

Belle cupped her hand over her mouth, trying not to laugh. "That's exactly what Donna used to say."

"Really?" replied Benji, embarrassed as she stabbed her fork into the fruit salad. She paused and looked at Belle.

"What's up? Did I say something wrong?" asked Belle.

"No, not at all. I was just wondering if you'd like some soda. I'm sure there's some in the fridge," said Benji as she looked back towards the building's open door.

Belle couldn't help but smile as she remembered Donna almost always asking the same thing. "No thanks," she replied.

Benji stood up and went into the kitchen as she called out to Grandma and asked if it was okay to take a soda.

"So long as you only take the cold ones, dear. And don't take any of the lemon ones. We're low on those, and Grandpa likes to save those for the end of the day."

"But Grandma, there's like, a whole bunch of lemon-flavoured ones in here."

"Oh, I guess he made a new batch. All right then, dear, take what you like."

Benji couldn't help but laugh at what Grandma said because the batch of lemon soda looked like it had been there quite a while, which made Benji think perhaps Grandpa didn't like the lemon ones all that much after all. It also made her wonder, if that *was* the case, what exactly happened to make Grandma think that Grandpa likes to save the lemon ones for the end of the day. Benji took one for herself, and even though Belle had declined, she took one for her anyway.

"Here you go," said Benji as she handed her a lemon soda. "I know you didn't ask for one, but I thought maybe in that space of time you may have changed your mind."

"Oh, okay. Thank you. I haven't changed my mind but thank you anyway. I'll save it for later."

"Okay. Hey, did I ever tell you about how Donna's dad once told me how he made his famous cordial?"

Belle smiled and raised an eyebrow as she thought back on the story Donna once told her about that exact same thing. "No, you didn't. Go ahead."

Unsurprised, Belle was told almost the exact same story by Benji that Donna once told her as they both sat there on those very same steps.

Belle ate. Benji drank. The conversation continued, and together they enjoyed what was left of the late-afternoon sun.

Finding an Old Pair of Shoes and Strolling to the Inconvenience Store

S abrina and her parents came home, and Sabrina trotted up the stairs to her room to change into a new set of clothes. As she opened her cupboard to decide what to wear, she noticed a pair of shoes.

Oh, she thought, *these shoes.*

She smiled as her thoughts wandered back to when her mother first bought those shoes and the kerfuffle it caused. The very same pair of shoes she wore to the convenience store the day Jacob banged his knee and he and her carted back to the village, thanks to Mr. Jones's kindness.

She put on the shoes, wondering to herself, "Huh. Has it really been that long?"

They didn't fit quite right. "Well, I guess I'm a growing girl. Didn't think I was growing *that* fast, though." Sabrina wriggled her feet into the shoes, then stomped each foot on the floor a few times, just to get her feet settled into the shoes. "Hm. That's not *too* bad, I guess."

Sabrina walked down the stairs, and her mother, having noticed her shoes, asked, "Honey, why are you wearing such an old pair of shoes?"

"Well, these are the same shoes you bought me a while ago. I wore them the same day Jacob and I carted back from the store, remember?"

"Oh, honey, no. That was this pair of shoes right here," replied her mother, pointing to a lone pair of shoes on a shoe rack under the stairs.

"Oh?" she said as she hurried down the stairs to see for herself.

As soon as she saw the shoes, she picked one of them up and looked at the shoes on her feet. "Huh. They're the same."

"Honey, you've been buying the same pair of shoes since we first moved to this town, and Jacob mentioned that he really like the shoes you were wearing. The pair on your feet right now is the second pair that are the same."

"But I thought—"

"It's okay, Sabrina. Sentimentality gets the best of all of us sooner or later."

"Oh," she said as she paused for a moment's thought. "Well," she said as she paused again. "I guess I'll just put these shoes on," she finished as she started to swap the shoes.

"And how are those shoes?" asked her mother.

"Oh my gosh, these shoes fit *so* much better," she said, relieved at the comfort they brought. "Oh, these *are* the shoes I wore to the store on that day with Jacob. Huh. Anyway, I'm off to the Inconvenience Store. I'll see you when I get back."

"See you, honey."

Out of habit, Sabrina headed off toward the front steps of the Town Dinner Hall where she often met Jacob before heading off to the Inconvenience Store. About halfway there, she realised what she was doing, stopped, paused for a moment's thought, and decided to go anyway since she might bump into someone who might like to join her on her walk.

Benji was stood at the bottom of the front steps of the Town Dinner Hall, twiddling her thumbs, pondering recent events, what life was like before them, and how life is going to have changed after them. As she heard the shuffling of feet approach, she looked up and saw Sabrina. "Oh, hi Sabrina. How are you today?"

"Actually, I was just about to head down to the Inconvenience Store if you'd like to join me."

Benji tilted her head slightly, smiled, thought about it for a second, and agreed. "Sure. I'd love to join you. It's not like I'm doing anything else anyway."

Sabrina and Benji both headed off, and happily and comfortably talked to each other about recent events, discussing what once was, what might have been, and what is yet to be.

"Oh," said Sabrina as they approached the old train station, "would you like to get something from the vending machine?"

"I honestly thought you might not want to go in there after everything that's happened."

"No, it's okay. I haven't been in there since it all happened anyway. I'd like to see how the construction workers have rebuilt the place."

"All right then."

They both walked into the station together, noting how improved and how much sturdier it seemed than before.

"Wow, and a new lick of paint too," noted Sabrina.

"Look at the vending machine," said Benji excitedly.

It was brand new. Newer than new. It shone and sparkled with the vibrancy of a clear, moonless, starlit night, and yet somehow was always the same old vending machine it had always been. "Oh, hey, Sabrina. Look at the drinks. They've got something written on them."

"Oh, they do. 'Share a drink with—'" Sabrina struggled to read further, as the words were wrapped around the can, and she couldn't quite see the last word. "Should we get one?"

"You can. I'd prefer to get something from the store."

"I'm too curious, plus I think the store would still be selling old stock and wouldn't have these in yet."

"Fair enough. It's up to you."

Sabrina inserted some coins into the machine and pushed the buttons for the drink she wanted. The machine buzzed and whirred, as the girls watched a mechanical arm collect a drink and drop it to the collection area. Sabrina knelt and retrieved the drink.

"What does it say?" smiled Benji, in hopes that it would be the name of a certain someone.

"'Share a drink with—' See for yourself," replied Sabrina as she turned the can around to show Benji.

"'Friends,'" said Benji as she saw the word. She smiled. "Appropriate."

Sabrina looked at Benji. Benji looked at Sabrina. They both smiled and continued on their way.

Forever

I t was a beautiful autumn day, as beautiful a day as there had ever been in the village. The sky was an immaculate blue, and the white and grey clouds spread from one horizon to another added to the beauty of an already lovely day.

Adam stepped out of the front door of his house onto the front porch and walked down the stairs as he decided to head over to Amanda's house.

As Adam walked across town, he smiled, waved, and had brief conversations with those he saw on the way, eventually arriving at Amanda's house.

"Knock, knock," called Adam as he knocked on Amanda's door. "Anyone home?"

"Oh, Adam. We're around the back," called Amanda.

Adam made his way around the back, where Amanda, Angela, Grandma, and Grandpa were all enjoying either a late breakfast or an early lunch.

"Ah, brunch. Mind if I join you?"

"Not at all, come sit down," said Amanda as she waved Adam over to join them. "So, what's up?"

"Uh, nothing. I'm actually feeling pretty good these days, but that doesn't mean I don't have a lot on my mind."

"You know what?" asked Grandpa. "It's perfectly fine to feel that way."

"Just still processing all of the things that have happened recently."

"You mean like that magic train ticket?" smirked Amanda.

"About that," said Adam as he patted his pockets, to try to find the ticket. "Would you know anything about this, Grandpa?" asked Adam as he pulled the ticket out of his top-left jacket pocket.

Everyone was shocked. It was more magnificent than Adam had described. It was a metallic, gold-coloured ticket that glowed with a molten-gold aura, and its aura pulsated as if it possessed a life of its own.

"It's mesmerising," said Angela.

"Can I have a look real quick?" Grandpa asked as he donned his glasses.

"By all means," said Adam as he handed over the ticket.

"Huh," said Grandpa as he inspected the ticket, front and back. "If this is what I *think* it is," began Grandpa, "you might wanna take it up to the train station from where you first arrived."

"I'll do that."

"And take Amanda with you," whispered Grandpa.

Adam nodded.

"What are we doing?" asked Amanda. "Did I just hear my name mentioned?"

Adam cleared his throat. "Well, actually, that brings me to why I came here in the first place. I was actually wondering if Amanda would like to join me for a walk to the train station."

"Sure. Any reason in particular?"

"For old time's sake. A stroll down memory lane, if you will."

"Sure. Let's pack this up, and we'll be on our way."

"Oh, no," interrupted Grandma, "we'll clear all of this up. You two be on your way. You don't mind, do you, Angela?"

"I don't mind at all."

"But, guys, this is *my* house. I can't expect you to—"

"Amanda, go," said Angela. "It's fine. Like Grandma said, we'll take care of this. Now, go." She shooed Amanda and Adam away from the table.

As Adam and Amanda walked to the train station, they used a whole lot of words to talk about a whole lot of nothing, enjoying the light split by the leaves of the trees.

Finally at the train station, the staff greeted Adam and Amanda with a friendly smile and a wave, and over by the vending machines, Adam noticed a glow similar to the one on his train ticket.

Adam walked over to the vending machine, the light pulsating more strongly the nearer he came. He took the ticket out of his pocket and inserted into the slot where money normally would go. The entire number pad lit up with the same glow as the ticket, only the hash and star symbols not lit.

Huh, thought Adam.

He reached to the keypad and pushed both unlit buttons at the same time. A mechanical whir and a soft *cher-clun*k later, and he kneeled down to extract whatever it was that the machine had given him. As he pulled it out, he was quite surprised to see just what it was.

"A wedding ring," he said inquisitively.

"Amanda," he said as she turned around, not realising he was still on bended knee.

"Adam," replied Amanda as he placed her hand on her chest in delighted shock. "Yes. I will. I do. I mean, yes."

Adam knelt there in stunned silence as he processed what had just happened. *Uh. Okay*, he thought. *Why not?*

"All right then," he said aloud. "It's decided."

"We're getting married," they both said in unison.

As Adam placed the ring on her finger, an impressive and intense amount of visions, past, present, and yet to come, flashed before both of them, each one aware of the other's experiences.

"Well, that was a heck of a thing," said Adam after the visions abruptly stopped.

"Agreed. And you know what?"

"Uh—I don't know. What?"

"What's the point in waiting?" she said, as she held up her hand and pointed to the ring.

"I guess none."

A few days passed, and Adam and Amanda stood at the altar, bride and groom. Vows exchanged, they shared a quick kiss and the congregation celebrated.

At the reception, Amanda turned her back to all the young girls and threw the bouquet of flowers. Everyone was surprised at how high it was thrown as they all reached for it. It landed with Sabrina. "Me? But I—me?"

"We're happy for you," said Benji while Belle nodded in agreement.

Sabrina stared blankly at them for a moment before she broke out laughing. "I guess I'm next then, huh?"

Various people happily talked amongst themselves before they all made their way to the train station to see off Adam and Amanda on their honeymoon.

On the train platform, the wedding guests all stood in row and handed the bride and groom envelopes, each one likely containing a sum of cash to help support them with their future; the one Belle handed them was notably different from the rest.

"Sorry. By the time I'd realised what was expected, I'd already made this one. I hope it's acceptable."

"Not a problem," said Adam as he took the envelope and pocketed it with all the others.

Adam and Amanda boarded the train and waved out the window as the train blew its whistle and left the station.

Adam got comfortable in his seat and looked upwards towards a beautiful blue sky where white and grey clouds drifted high above the treetops, while a gentle breeze blew softly through the woodlands. He saw a leaf carried by the breeze dance to the song of the wind as it called through the trees, gently descending towards an unbeaten path.

Epilogue

Belle and Benji became as close as Belle and Donna ever were and as close as two friends could ever be.

Sabrina and Angela became so close that Angela become like a second mother to Sabrina.

Grandma and Grandpa continued to live ordinary lives, helping out wherever and whenever they could.

Max and Julie became successful street performers, performing in the city once a week.

Joshua remained a vagabond, wandering from town to town, living one day at a time, never knowing where his next meal was coming from.

Kevin eventually acquired a job in the city and moved there permanently, which made him grow distant from the village, the people, and the lives they led there.

Donna was never found.

It was just after dusk; the train's motion had rocked Amanda to sleep, and for some reason Adam couldn't quite take his mind off how different the envelope Belle had given him felt. He rummaged around his top-left jacket pocket, searching for Belle's envelope. He took it out and was delighted by the card, surprised by the amount of money she'd gifted them, and shocked by the message she'd written: *I'm pregnant. You're the father.*

THE END

Acknowledgements

My development editor, Carrie Jones, for her passion and excitement for the world I've created, and for helping me develop that world from a somewhat slapped-together novella into a full-blown novel. Her enthusiasm gave me the drive I needed to keep writing.

My cover illustrator, Meritxell Andreu (character design; colouring), and her collaborator, Ferran Rodríguez (train station design) for bringing the world I've created into the visual medium.

My copy editor and proof reader, Joe Pierson, for simplifying a lot of my sentences without sacrificing their meaning, and catching all the little things everyone else missed.

The website *Reedsy.com*, where I was able to hire the aforementioned people

The website *Draft2Digital*, where I was able to self-publish this novel.

Don't miss out!

Visit the website below and you can sign up to receive emails whenever Ian Anthony Hollis publishes a new book. There's no charge and no obligation.

https://books2read.com/r/B-A-LQUK-EHNWB

BOOKS 2 READ

Connecting independent readers to independent writers.

Also by Ian Anthony Hollis

The Cities & Villages Saga
In a Small, Quiet Village (Where Nothing Much Ever
Happens)

Standalone
And so Began the War

About the Author

Born and raised in Port Macquarie, New South Wales (NSW), Australia, Ian is a well-travelled English language teacher whose favourite hobbies are music, movies, video games and the internet. Ian dreams of one day being a filmmaker.